"DON'T ROCK...
THE BOAT!"

Harvey Price

Publisher: Harvey L. Price Jr.
Hoquiam, Washington

ISBN: 978-0-9819220-4-1

Library of Congress Control Number: 2009905760

Back cover: Image Credit: "Earthrise", NASA Image AS8-14-2383. Photo taken on Dec. 24, 1968, by William Anders on Apollo 8 mission.

Front cover: Lake Billy Chinook. Photo taken by author-2008.

Interior image: "Suricata" is licensed under Creative Commons Attribution Shared Alike 1.0 License.

"Old Persian Cuneiform Alphabet", found in the Article Inspector's "The Secret of Numbers" by Amir Nouri.

Printed by Minuteman Press, Olympia, Washington, and bound by Phil's Bindery, Seattle, Washington.

FOR

KATHREEN LOUISE

AND

SHARYN

ACKNOWLEDGEMENT

It is not possible to undertake a project like writing a book without having the help and support of special people in your life. And I am blessed to have such. Without them, my boat most certainly would have capsized long ago. Each of these individuals have helped guide and steady me throughout my own voyage.

Four, in particular, gave life to this book. As with each book that I have written before this, Tom and Liz Hicker provided countless hours of review, suggestions and needed changes. The amazing talents of Jeanne Saville gave the story a much-needed scrubbing and re-direction. Her perspective and comments were invaluable.

And Jeannie gives me the gravitational force to help keep me earthbound. Without her, I am sure that I would have drifted aimlessly up and away into the endless void of space.

"Merrill"

Photo by Murial Gottrop (April, 2005).
Shepherd's staff added by author.

FOREWARD

It seems appropriate before retelling the ancient accounts about Noah, The Flood and of his ark, to acknowledge that at no time in this story has it been meant to mock any set of beliefs. On the contrary, the attempt has been to try and take what is recorded of these events in the Bible's Old Testament, as found in the Appendix of this book, and simply expand on them somewhat...from the soon-to-be confined animals' and birds' perspectives.

The ancient story of The Flood is one of the most revered and often retold in all recorded history. What follows now is simply a minor expansion of how it might have unfolded. Wherever possible, every attempt has been made to faithfully describe what might have happened, given the information recorded in the Genesis account. And just maybe by doing so, this might suggest to any potential reader some parallels to our present day world. Certainly we, today, are all facing a rash of significant changes around us, most of which seem to be the result of our collective behaviors and actions.

My hope is that you proceed to read what follows. In doing so, it might help to remind each of us to work harder at being less careless...with others, with our world, and, as Merrill would implore us, with the animals and birds who also live here among us. We are presently rocking our boat, and it could possibly capsize if we do not pay attention to how rough the restless seas are becoming.

CONTENTS

APPENDIX

x

THE PRESENT DAY

ONE: GETTING ACQUAINTED

This is tough, and I'm just not sure how best to begin...

Before you learn about the remarkable discovery I just unearthed, it might be helpful if I started with a brief introduction and some personal, background information.   Otherwise,   you'll probably never believe what I'm about to tell you.

First off, and as difficult as it is to believe, I'm a meerkat. Yep, that's one of my extremely distant relatives who you've just seen before reading this page. As you saw, I'm a four-legged creature, who is rather sparsely covered with odd-clumps of bristly hair, who appears to always be looking nervously about with beady eyes; and who has a short, pointed nose and matted-down ears. We're an odd study in vigilance, even if in my case I have lost much of that edge.

BUT, I can speak and even write. So that's got to be something in my favor. However, as I have recently found out, having those abilities didn't used to be such a big deal. But in today's world, for me to have these capabilities, and if it were known that I did, I'm sure that I would be considered a strange aberration, a "freak of nature", as you're so fond of saying. So for obvious reasons, I don't broadcast them. Besides, not even my closest relatives know, nor does anyone else in either the animal or the avian kingdoms. You are the first to be told. And I am, as far as I know, the last of a kind. But, as I have already alluded to, it wasn't always the way it is now.

That said, you probably might shrug and ask, "How, then, do you maintain these skills?"

I do so mostly by talking to myself, writing odd notes and keeping diaries, which as it turns out, is apparently a genetic trait, another one that I just recently found out about. But my writing is not like anything you're used to seeing or reading. As far as I can tell, it predates anything, anyone has ever seen. And as far as talking, I don't; except to myself. I only listen to others. No one would let me begin talking to them, without probably becoming overly excited. So, this limits me to sneaking into civic auditoriums, movie theaters, college and university campus venues, church sanctuaries and choir lofts and listening to what others have to say, play or sing.

"Do I have a name?" you most probably might inquire next.

No, I don't. Why would I need one? The only way my kinfolk communicate with me or one another is using clicks, barks and snorts. If I were to one day yell out, "Enough, already! Would you please stop with the guttural noises! Just say what you mean!", I'd have my relatives and neighbors dashing into their burrows and locking their doors in sheer panic. Or if I were to call out to a prey that I was chasing, "Will you give it a break?! I'm simply exhausted from all this running. And besides, you're not THAT tasty!" I'd have creatures near and far clearing out of here, leaving me with no dining options or variety. And "yes", it's true; I and my kind do dine on others. We are, after all, considered to be carnivores...nobody's perfect.

So where then does this leave us?... Oh, yes, "where do I live?" you might wonder.

In the Sinai Desert for the most part. Occasionally, I will migrate into the Dead Sea region, especially during the height of the winter season. It's just a nice change of pace for me. But even more significant than my coming to this vacation retreat on a personal whim, this same area around the Dead Sea became my very distant relative's second, major habitat...after *the beginning of the Second Beginning*; or stated another way, as this upcoming story will later unfold, after *the end of the First Beginning*. However, there eventually arose so much human-type activity in this area that over time my forbearers shifted further south into the Sinai to avoid the onslaught of surging armies, ones that seemed unceasingly preoccupied with a wanting to kill each other...talk about ME being strange...

But the setting now, for me to tell you this most amazing story, one that I have just been

3

privileged enough to find, is deep inside one of the old, cave-like structures on a cliff face, overlooking the Dead Sea. My guess is that it isn't too far from where some of your kind found those Dead Sea Scrolls some years ago. But what I stumbled upon were not scrolls, and they were not in a cave.

What I found were tablets, hundreds of them, all stacked neatly in orderly rows. They were buried deep inside an immense burrow, one that none of my relatives had ever discovered before. For me, it was simply happenstance. Actually, I was lost. But it was the most amazing discovery, and how it all survived these thousands upon thousands of years, I'll never know.

The tablets were imprinted in a pre-cuneiform script, in a language that no one, other than some wandering meerkat like me, might even vaguely understand. At that, it took me many months to refresh my deciphering skills to be able to interpret it. By doing so, what follows next is the remarkable account of what was written on those tablets. Periodically, I may insert a comment, which will always be enclosed in a bracket, e.g. [ed. note: …]. My hope is that by adding these comments, it may help to clarify, translate or enhance what was written so long ago. In addition, you will find that the author wrote some comments in *italics*, which I assume was a way to indicate that they were his own personal or editorial thoughts. And finally, this same author wrote anything directly related to The Deity in **bold** script.

All that said; now prepare yourself for a shock.

THE COMMISSION

TWO: THE WORLD AS IT WAS

Well, at least there wasn't mold in this place. If there was ever a case for the Floodmaster being mindful of unintended consequences, covering the planet with water for over a year is one. Not only was there mold, fungus and slime everywhere or in everything, there was nothing but seafood to eat. I'd given just about anything for a nice, crisp scorpion to gnaw on during those earlier times.

Oh yeah! Before I go any further, you need to know that my name is Merrill. And my much better half's name is Holly. We're actually two of a parade of animals and birds that fairly recently have been released from quarantine. It wasn't like we all had some kind of disease. However, that's not to say the people that used to live around us before our boat trip didn't. Without a doubt, they were frightfully infected with something. And how do I know?

Probably a little background information

might help with that answer. You see, Holly and I are both meerkats. That means we are part of the mongoose family, which in turn means we have little fear of your most venomous snakes. Recognizing that about us, the folks where we used to live, somewhere that is hundreds, if not thousands, of miles south of where we now find ourselves, encouraged folks like Holly and I to live close by. They actually fed us. Why? It was because we kept the snake population in check. (To me, there's nothing like eating sun-baked, broiled or mostly dead snake in the morning to make you feel alive!) Anyway, living close by them like we did, we saw and heard lots about the people who lived around us.

And most of it wasn't very good.

It appeared that life in those times had become brittle and testy. Nobody, it seemed, was satisfied simply having what they needed to be reasonably comfortable. And by that I mean housed in relative comfort and safety; clothed adequately for whatever changes the weather might bring and nourished on a regular basis, enough so, anyway, to stay healthy. Instead, it seemed to Holly and I, perched, ever-vigilant on the sidelines, there was always a mad scramble to acquire, by any means, what anyone else had that you didn't. And those items ranged from trinkets, money, food, someone else's land, family possessions or treasures, to wives, husbands and even their children.

It got so bad that the meanest of these "accumulators", as we called them, began to capture and collect folks like us. Everything was being grabbed or in immediate danger of being taken. Vast amounts of possessions became the sought-after markers of a successful life. The more you had, the more successful you were. And the bigger the possessions were, the better you were. It was madness, run amuck.

And helping to make all this craziness available to anyone hoping to join this endless cycle of accumulation were those who we call the "facilitators". They were individuals who became the lackeys to the most powerful of the "accumulators". In the facilitator group, there were the "money changers" as they were called then [ed. note: Like the investment bankers of today. And be advised, as I mentioned earlier, being the discoverer and official editor of these tablets, I will be interjecting comments from time to time. They could include clarifications, comparisons or just reinforcing comments. In this first instance, it is simply for contemporary comparison.]; and the "quislings", those who supposedly represented the people who were constantly being duped and misrepresented [ed. note: ...corrupt politicians today.]. The worst of the accumulators were the "warlords" and the bands of their henchmen [ed. note: ...dictators and terrorists today.]. And the last major group in this sad downturn of our earlier world was most of the general population [ed. note: ...the silent and fearful majority today], who were desperately trying to maintain some order in their lives the only way they knew how, fearful acquiesce to the will of the all-powerful.

And to maintain the populace in this

indentured state, the various powers came up with the idea of using credit to keep the masses forever beholding to them. It was highly successful and terribly demoralizing. Between the greed of the more powerful and the indebtedness of everyone else, the world became filled with an almost, self-destructive hopelessness.

Then next, you might ask, how did this all begin? The truth is; I haven't a clue. But it does appear as Holly and I observed more and more of everyone's behavior, it was like there were no-see-ums always buzzing about inside the heads of so many people. And as they buzzed around inside there, the infected populations' choices and decisions became crazier and crazier. For instance, the message was circulated far and wide that your home was really just an investment; its value would continue to increase indefinitely. So why not borrow against that so-called increasing value and buy things you didn't need. Likewise, these same powers issued cards, ones which didn't require you to pay back what you owed immediately and would allow you to purchase, unchecked, more unneeded items on credit. This cycle of debt became epidemic and catastrophic; the more it increased, the more desperate and hopeless the entire population became. Conflict was everywhere. And all Holly and I could do was observe this process unfolding. That was until one day when we were approached by our closest neighbor, an oversized gentlemen who everyone called "Noah".

At that time Noah and his extended family, along with Holly and I, lived in an area south of the equator. And from what I understood, by way of my ongoing conversations with migrating birds that occasionally stopped by our local delta, it was a massive landmass that all of us either lived on or flew over. We called this super-continent "Pangaea". And the area we lived in was near the Okavango Delta, close to the Okavango River. [ed note: You will find this area in the present day Kalahari Basin, surrounding the smaller Kalahari Desert, in the South Africa nation of Botswana.] It was a region filled to overflowing with the richest variety of plants, animals and birds, large and small. The red, volcanic soil was richly fertile, and the weather was absolutely perfect for every living thing to thrive in this magnificent land. Unfortunately for all of us, the only exception was that the people didn't. To me, they seemed lost.

All our meerkat ancestors and relatives came from this area. As Holly and I are still proud to say, we were some of this region's first inhabitants. And unlike what sadly seems to be occurring after the *"Second Beginning"*, during those earlier times all animals and birds could speak, and a few of us, including yours truly, could even write. However, given the awful mess people made of the *"First Beginning"*, Noah predicted to Holly and I, that some day he spoke to us, there probably was no longer going to be the totally free exchange of ideas that all of us once had. Over time, he surmised, animals and birds will be condemned to expressing themselves with chortles, peeps, grunts, roars, barks and occasional singing. But no conversation will likely be possible. And we didn't even cause this cock up!! Where's the justice in all that? After his remarks, I vowed I'd definitely like to find a world without people, and then let's see how well we animals and birds could do running things ourselves.

Anyway, like a bad case of mange, people came along sometime after animals and birds had developed peaceful and productive relationships. And very soon, as we were about to learn, because of their innate ability to foul everything up, almost as if there was some kind of grand prize for doing so, most of them, corrupt and honest alike, were about to take a fast and wet exit.

THREE: THE **FLOODMASTER'S** INSTRUCTIONS

Now, if the truth be told, Noah was known in our local circle of critters as someone who wasn't always connecting all the dots evenly. For example, he kept going around and telling everyone he was 600 years old! [ed. note: And then when you read further in Genesis that he eventually lived to the very, ripe old age of 950 years, you realize he was still in his prime at 600.] Give me a break! I can tell a yarn as good as anyone, but the first rule of yarns is make them halfway believable. But he was a good man, even if he couldn't count.

So, picture if you will, Holly and I taking our turn at being on lookout for the family, who at that time were all sleeping underground in our cozy burrow. We were doing our usual routine of looking in all directions, being ever-alert, for what, I never could quite figure out. There certainly weren't any hostiles in our neighborhood, and people usually stayed clear of us, except for a visit from Noah now and then. It was just out of habit, I guessed. And then it was Holly that noticed that

Noah was walking purposefully in our direction. By the time he hurriedly arrived, he was somewhat out of breath and called out to us, wheezing as he did.

"Merrill, Holly, I urgently need to speak to you both," he gasped. Pausing to gulp down a few more breaths, he then added, "I've have been given some earth-shaking instructions from **God** that are overwhelming, and I need help...lots of it!"

"What's up?" I asked, thinking that maybe his wife had put her foot down about how poorly he was keeping his garden these days. There are, after all, some benefits to telling everyone you're over 500 years old. You can feign fatigue, forgetfulness or painful flatulence and avoid most household chores. But something told me it wasn't the Missis. that issued these latest instructions. He seemed quite overwhelmed.

"First off," he began, "Do you know where I can find about 20,000 board feet of gopher wood?" [ed. note: See the accompanying Appendix: "THE OLD TESTAMENT'S GENESIS ARK STORY", Genesis 6:14-16.]

"20,000 board feet!" I exclaimed. "What are you building? A city? And **Who** would be asking you to get that amount of wood? Forget it! Just tell **Whoever** it is to get it themselves. And then afterwards, **He** or **She** can come back; and you can talk. Also, while you're at it, you can tell **Whoever** gave you the instructions that you've never heard of 'gopher wood'; it doesn't exist, at least anywhere in these parts. It sounds to me like **Whoever** this is will have you packing up soon to

12

go on a snipe hunt. This has to be a joke."

"No, Merrill, it doesn't work that way," Noah said, dipping his head slightly, as if he were becoming progressively overwhelmed at what lay ahead. "I have to do what I am told. The matter is ominously serious, and my instructions are non-negotiable."

"Well, then, if that's the case, what exactly are you supposed to do with all this wood?" I pressed.

"Build an ark with three decks," came the surprising reply.

"Sorry," I answered, "but I have to ask, what's an ark?"

"Oh!" he apologized, "I thought you knew; it's like a boat."

"Ok, then if that's the case, with that amount of wood, it's going to be a huge boat. Just how big is it supposed to be anyway?"

"300 cubits by 50 cubits by 30 cubits."

"You know, as poorly as I'm grasping your message, I've still got to ask another question: what's a cubit?"

And it was about then I had decided that it was really past time for me to begin scratching around something to eat for breakfast. It was obvious to me that this conversation was going nowhere.

"It's the distance from the tip of your elbow to the tip of your middle or longest finger," Noah proudly replied, as if it was at least something he had some knowledge about and control over.

"It strikes me there could be some variation

in that measurement," I cautioned. "If you use your arm versus mine, you will have a wide margin for error. What if, when you're building this boat of yours, everyone that helps uses their own particular 'cubits' to measure by? Or say you just used my own cubit. You sure wouldn't need 20,000 board feet of lumber! But if you use your cubit, I bet it will take all of that or more…provided you can ever find any gopher wood. But **Who** was it, anyway, that told you to do all this?"

"It was **God**," he answered promptly and gravely again.

"Well, I hate to keep compounding your miseries, but I must ask **Who** or **What** is **God**?"

"It was **God** who created the heavens and the earth and all that dwells therein," he replied with great solemnity.

"It didn't just happen?!!" I asked with some genuine amazement.

"Nope. **God** did it all."

*Now, let me take a minute for a break away from this revelation and breaking news feature. It was at that moment I had heard about all I could process in one entire lifetime, much less in the space of two minutes. Here was this fellow, who obviously couldn't count how long he'd been alive, coming to two rather worn and weary ground-dwellers and asking us to help him find, at the very least, 20,000 board feet of a then unknown tree, so that he could immediately start building a boat of undeterminable size because it has to be measured in 'cubits', which **Someone** named "**God**" had told him to do, because this "**God**" had already made* *everything else to begin with. It was just too much. I felt like saying, "You must be joking. You're such a big kidder, Noah."*

So, gradually I collected myself and looked over at Holly, who by this time was rolling her eyes in our private code, which meant that we were having another exciting and bewildering encounter with a human and that she was slipping into our burrow to get some daily chores started. It signaled that she felt this conversation was going nowhere. She had more important duties to attend to...like sleeping.

Giving her a reassuring hug, indicating I was in complete agreement, while simultaneously nodding to imply that neighbors are neighbors and that I should at least try to hear the gentleman out, I then turned to Noah and began my summary of what I understood him to have said.

"Chief," I started, "I'm going to propose that your first issue, that of you having to locate this 'gopher wood' is a matter of confusing an adjective with a verb. You're being instructed to 'go for' some wood. What kind of wood you build anything with is entirely up to you and it depends on what's available in our area. My suggestion is that you begin with that Yellowwood grove of trees that's just up from your largest barn, next to your largest pasture, and which extends halfway up the hillside. You could even build your so-called 'cubit' boat in the pasture area next to that forest. But I'd stay away from the Ironwood trees that are scattered throughout the area. If you start chewing away at one of those, you'll be working at it for weeks.

Stay with the softer woods.

"Next, I'd suggest you standardize your measurements a little more precisely than using 'cubits'. Some of us here, locally, have been fooling around with using 'inches' or 'centimeters'. And there is quite an ongoing debate, even as we speak, as to which one is best. My preference is inches and feet, particularly for the job you've apparently been assigned to complete. It's one thing to build a wooden boat, but if you were to build a metal one, which would be much more difficult, particularly since we haven't discovered anything yet to do so with, then you'd probably have to use our more precise and scientifically-based metric system. Indeed, with this upcoming job, you're only going to be able to use axes, hammers and trowels. All and all, I'd go with inches."

"So, what's an 'inch'?" the elderly gentleman inquired, appearing somewhat relieved at how practically this conversation was progressing.

"It's the length of any average adult meerkat's largest, claw-shaped toe. And one foot is twelve of these inches, the exact length of the distance between an average, adult meerkat's front and rear legs, when he or she is standing perfectly still. In addition, if Holly or I were to take three hops, that equals three feet or one yard. Knowing all this, you can then appreciate the many other measurements, which various ones of us in the animal and bird kingdom use, for instance: the 'Ja' is 12 inches; the 'Gudge' is 27 inches; the 'Sen' is 43.74 yards; the 'Ungul' is 0.75 inch; the 'Zhang' is

3.45 yards' the 'Fathom' is 6 feet; and the 'Acre' is 4,840 yards.

"Taking this a step further, if you convert your **Big Boss**' instructions, using your own 'cubit' as a guide, which I would guess, without actually measuring it, is very close to 24 inches from the tip of your own elbow to the tip of your middle finger, your boat is going to be 600 feet long, 100 feet wide, and 60 feet high. Area-wise, if you're looking at four decks, including the top deck, that will come to a total storage area of 5.45 acres. [ed. note: Stated another way: their ark will be two football fields long, or a little over half the length of a Nimitz-Class Aircraft Carrier, which is 1,049 feet in length. And it will be a little less than the width of said Carrier, through its 134 foot beam.] What could you want to put inside- and on top of- something that big?!!!"

"Seven pair of so-called 'clean' animals and fowl and a pair each of all the other animals and birds that exist, plus all the seeds or starter shoots of plants that grow anywhere," came his stunning answer.

Following that startling revelation, both of us were totally silent for about five minutes, each considering for the first time the immense implications of what both of us had just said. There was only one word that finally came to mind after the shock diminished, enough at least that I could speak.

"Why?"

"Because there is going to be a flood," Noah almost whispered, as if he did not want anyone else to hear.

"So," I retorted, almost relieved, "we've had some pretty big rain storms here in the past, and occasionally there was some minor flooding. I don't see anything about this weather prediction to get our knickers in a stitch about. We can easily handle a little heavier-than-usual rainfall."

"For forty days and forty nights, non-stop?!!" Noah countered."This is not going to be like anything, anyone, anywhere, ever witnessed or experienced. The flood water will cover everything!"

"Who was this you were talking to, again?" I asked, a bit more meekly this time around.

"**The Creator of the Heavens and the Earth**, of all the fish and fowl and other life thereon. And there was no mincing of words. It was not an invitation or a discussion. They were commands and revelations from **The Most High**."

"How did this **Floodmaster** appear to you?" I could now only feebly continue asking. "How could you be so convinced you weren't having a really bad dream, maybe even hallucinating on some, old, dried mushroom, or probably seeing a talking mirage? It had to be a mistake. How could anything and everything be so bad that it all has to be drowned? And why are you coming to Holly and I with this? Look at me, I'm just a flea-scratching, rat-haired appearing, ground-burrow-smelling, snake and scorpion-eating varmint."

"That's true," Noah concurred, nodding as he agreed with me. "You are all that. But you and Holly will be invaluable to the success of this effort.

You move freely and quickly, if not quite nervously at times, amongst all the animals and birds in this land. Most seem to respect you; and, at least, all that could, don't seem to dine on you. Even the ones you eat don't seem to hold too many grudges. In addition, you can speedily organize sending this urgent message everywhere and organize this overwhelming assembly, while my family and I start building the 'ark', as it will be called henceforth by me. Quite likely, we will need to have some of the animals help with the construction and heavy lifting, once the selection process is underway. I will be talking to you more about that later.

"And as to how this commission was delivered to me; it was a **Voice** only. But along with it came such an overwhelming aura of **Authority** and **Presence**. There was no doubt left as to **Who** was speaking. If you should ever have the opportunity to hear it, you will know what I mean."

"Does that mean I'm just supposed to take your word for it? Possibly, I can muster up enough trust in you to go along with this, but I'm not so sure my animal and bird brothers and sisters will do the same as me. Maybe I could make it sound like a raffle or lottery and whoever wins gets a boat trip of a lifetime, but even that won't entice everyone. Or maybe I could say the whole planet is going to be destroyed of all life, and have a contest to see who could run or fly the fastest across a finish line and thereby be saved. Or possibly I could simply tell them what you've told me and have them discuss it within their own kind, each choosing seven pairs, and then wait to see if things get hairy. Frankly, I'm not sure if I want to be the one who tells a particular party that they are not 'clean'. Everyone will just have to hang out around the boat while you put the finishing touches on it. And if or when the weather gets really nasty, maybe they'll select amongst themselves who will climb aboard. Of the three options, the last one seems the best. What say you?"

"I'd say the latter option. You have to be honest about all this. Let each individual group or species decide within their own body how they want to react to this news," Noah answered. "It quite honestly could be a grand case of 'they built a city, or in this case a very large ark, but nobody came to sail on it'.

"And speaking of which, I have one other favor to ask of you."

"What's that?" I asked, by now filled with the dread of the ages. *I could only just barely imagine what could follow his last series of announcements and requests.*

"Would you please try to come up with some ideas on a design for the ark? What do I know about ships, boats or arks? I'm a farmer."

"Well, take another hard look at me," I responded. "Do I look like a shipwright? I've never even seen a boat! To tell you the truth, I have a very uneasy feeling about this whole venture. Somehow, the cast involved just doesn't seem to be the right mix. Is there any way you can contact the **Commissioner of this Catastrophe**, and see if any changes in personnel or in this plan is possible?"

"Not a chance," Noah replied. "It was clear and final what I was told. Now it's up to us to get it done."

"Us?... Was my name mentioned in all this discussion and issuing of orders? It now appears you have invoked the 'Royal We' in your preliminary preparations for this venture."

"Quite possibly so," came the not so reassuring confirmation. "A job has to be done and you and Holly are now drafted into the growing ranks of participants. I admit it isn't fair and that it won't be easy; but by now you've already noticed that much of life isn't. Your help is needed. The three of us have no choice."

"Well, all I can say to what you've just told me is that I need to take a break and talk to Holly. We'll discuss your requests and see what we come up with. For now, it appears to me you're going to have your hands full cutting down half that forest adjacent to your farm's largest pasture. You'd best get started with that chore. I might suggest after you cut the trees, you start shaping them into cants, twelve inches square and one hundred feet long. You're going to need hundreds of them. In the meantime, I'll talk to Holly; and we'll catch up with you and your family in a day or so."

"That was kind of my thinking as well," Noah acknowledged. "Before anything else can be done, we've got to start getting the building materials together. Then there is the matter of supplies."

"STOP!! I don't want to hear it...!! Leave

it be. Try working on one thing at a time. Take some deep breaths and work off some of that anxiety chopping down trees and shaping some logs. And I'll see you in a few days with our answers to your requests."

CONSTRUCTION AND CONFUSION

FOUR: NOAH'S BOX

What has happened to this point and what follows is taken from the diaries that I and my lifetime partner kept for almost two years. We can only hope the tablets we recorded it all on will stay safe and undisturbed until the right party finds them. There is no way we will know how long it will be before someone does, but we sincerely hope they are in good enough condition to read when it happens. Heaven, and all who are therein, knows it took us long enough to prepare them. The events that are recorded, as mentioned previously, took about two years, but for us to record them has taken us another seven. But it kept us busy, intermixed between starting our family, a life-long desire of ours that was prematurely interrupted by the events that we describe herein. And to complete this seemingly impossible task, Holly organized a chapter and then I proceeded to write it. If we hadn't done it that way, this project would have taken one of us longer than either of us had to live on this still-soggy planet.   Now, to resume recording the world's spiral into a totally unpredictable future...

After our first flood-related conversation, I stood silently for a while watching old man Noah amble back to his farm, which was actually the nicest one in the area, as far as I could tell. His wife, Nora, and his three sons, Ham, Shem and Japheth and their families were the most industrious in the region. They cultivated acres and acres of crops, planted sturdy trees along its border to provide wind-breaks for the fruit and nut trees, and had all manner of livestock and fowl. When each son would marry, a new home was built on adjoining property that Noah had set aside for that purpose. And each son and their wives had the same dedication and perseverance to farm, cultivate and husband their land and family as Nora and Noah did. All told, Nora and Noah had at least seventeen or eighteen grandchildren, some old enough to soon start their own families.

All of their farms were located in a valley just below where Holly and I lived. The surrounding hillsides were covered with a thick forest of old growth yellowwood trees. And coursing through their farms was a stream that flowed throughout the year. It provided them all the water that they and their animals and crops needed. Bordering each side of the stream were their individual family plots, dotted with log cabin-like dwellings. This isn't deep desert, you know. Our neighbors don't have to always be sleeping in tents or moving from here to there to get food or water.

After all, in Noah's 600 years he's had ample time to build whatever permanent structures he needed. Even I could have built something substantial to live in, given that amount of time; rather than always having to live underground.

And finally, each of their farms is cross-fenced for protecting and breeding their various herds of animals and flocks of birds.

And it was not too long after that first meeting with Noah when Holly and I had some lunch and then climbed outside our home to rest and to continue our discussion about what Noah had told me. After my detailing what he said, she began to outline what she thought had to be done. Frankly, it never ceased to amaze me how she could take any emergency or unforeseen event and make the most of it.

So, for you, the individual who finds these tablets one day, what is now written on them is what Holly and I transcribed from the initial notes we wrote and kept in our burrow and from the log I kept on the Wheel House wall for over a year. As with that first conversation with Noah, it will be word-for-word what was done and said.

"Merrill, honey," Holly began, "this is what I think you need to do next. Go down below here and get something to take notes on, while I dictate to you in broad terms what it will take to build this boat you've just described to me. I'll wait until you get back up topside to begin."

Hurrying to get what I needed, I quickly climbed back out and perched myself on a rock outside our burrow's entrance. Holly sat on one a little above me, gazing out over the landscape below, but focusing mostly on the pasture next to the woods adjacent to Nora and Noah's property.

"I'll begin with the keel section of Noah's boat," she started. "And as you mentioned to me earlier, and I agree, most timbers need to be 100 feet long, particularly those that are to be used for the keel, bottom deck and as supports for the next three decks, including the top deck. To reduce some unnecessary labor, the keels can be three-sided cants, as you have already instructed them to begin shaping. The fourth side can be left rough with the bark still in place. For the keel, there needs to be 90 of these cut and shaped into 24 inch-square cants. And they will be assembled in five separate, 600 foot-long groups, with rows of three cants in each of six, 100 foot sections. The middle of each section is to be staggered, starting with a 50 foot length, then alternated with 100 foot ones every other 50 foot beam. All three are to be secured together with tie rods at twenty foot intervals, using straight tree limbs, driven through already bored holes and fastened at each end, through each beam. One of these three-beam assemblies are to be at each outside edge of the length of the 600 foot boat and the others are to be attached at 25 foot intervals across the width of the keel.

"Overlaying these five separate keel sections will be attached, crosswise, 100 foot, 12 inch-square cants; but these have to be squared on all four sides. You will need 600 of these to lay the bottom deck floor, and then they, in turn, will have tie rods drilled and pegged into each of the five keel lengths to secure this decking to the keel logs. In addition, at each end of these 600 beams, they will need to have mortise holes chiseled-out, which are four inches square by four inches deep. The two sides of the boat will eventually be secured inside these holes. Plus, on the first and six hundredth beams, each needs to have these same holes bored or cut out every 12 inches for the 100, 12 inch-square, upright cants, which will form the stern and bow of the boat.

"The next three decks will be 20 feet above each other. The fourth and final deck will, of course, be topside. There will be 24 inch-square cants used as floor joists, placed every ten feet along the boat's 600 foot length. They, too, need to be 100 feet long, and will have 4 inch tenons cut at each end to fit into the upright cants, which will have 4 inch mortises cut in them, every 20 feet on their 60 foot length. But these mortises will only be every 10 feet along the length of the boat. Underneath each 24 inch square beam will be a 12 inch triangle wedge secured to the side beam to provide extra support for each joist.

"As already mentioned, the cants for the boat's sides will be 12 inch square, 60 foot lengths, as will be those for the bow and stern. All these timbers will definitely want to be three-sided cants, with the rough side facing outward."

"But this will give Noah's boat the appearance of a giant, floating, tree stump!" I exclaimed. "I prefer it look more like a ship with some smooth, curved lines or maybe like a yacht or at least like one that didn't look like a piece of oversized driftwood. What will anyone think who sees this thing bobbling by?"

"Who, for instance?" Holly quietly reminded me. "Isn't the whole idea of this ark is that there aren't going to be any bystanders or well-wishers along the way? We're it, as I understand what you've been told."

"Yeah, I see your point," I acknowledged, saddened by the full realization of what she was saying. "I guess I was just hoping for something a little more stylish looking than a bark-covered box to save the remnants of civilization and every plant, animal and bird species in the world. But go on, what next do you envision needs to be done?"

"Overlaying the next two upper decks, above the bottom or fourth deck, there will have to be staggered timbers, which should be 4 inches thick, 11 inches wide and 20 feet long. They will have to be secured to the joists by wooden pegs; there being no other way to fasten them. By using this width, there will be a one inch space between each timber. [ed. note: Remember: there is no metal; therefore, they have no nails.] The top deck, however, will have to have 12 inch-wide boards, which will eliminate any gaps and will help ensure it is waterproof. That deck, the bottom one, and each of the four sides have to be thoroughly pitched to prevent leaks. And in the middle of each of these three decks, there will have to be a 10 foot by 10 foot hole cut and a ramp built to extend down to the next deck level. A Ramp House will have to be built over the top deck's opening, as well as a door to cover it, in the event of foul weather or rough seas."

"Foul weather and rough seas?" I stopped my recording suddenly and shot a concerned glance at her. "Who said anything about having those? I thought it was just supposed to be lots of rain and then possibly an extended boat ride thereafter. No one mentioned 'rough seas' to me! Look at me! I can't swim!! I've never even seen a body of water larger than our creek below us. I hardly even drink water! I like our burrow; it's dry and safe. 'Foul weather and rough seas' sound nothing like dry or safe. Maybe it's time for me to talk to Noah."

"Calm yourself, Merrill," my foresighted and all-knowing partner countered. "I'll be there. It will be ok. If we can get the boat built to these specifications, it should be seaworthy and safe. And that leaves me just a couple more aspects of this boat to discuss with you.

"The top deck should have some kind of railing that encircles it, except for a 12 foot gap, where a gate will be built immediately in front of the ramp opening on the top deck. And at the bow of the boat, when it is finished, there needs to be a small Wheel House built, which will include a 24 square inch, forward-facing window. I'll talk more about what could go inside the Wheel House later. And finally on this upper deck, there needs to be a roped-off section at the stern. Behind it will be a series of four, Restroom Facilities. One of them needs to be at least 10 feet wide, to accommodate the larger animals; and one, slightly smaller one, will have no roof to accommodate the taller ones. One will be for people only, and the fourth one will be for smaller creatures like us. Further, to the stern of these four houses, wooden sluices will be installed, each one extending a good eight feet beyond the stern railing of the boat, and angled downward 10 degrees. These Restroom Facilities are for everyone to use. There are to be no exceptions, except for the birds that can fly, once it is possible to do so. All others who cannot, including chickens, must use these facilities EXCLUSIVELY!!"

"Oh, I see," I said, feeling for once in tune with her train of thought. "This will be our poop deck!"

To which, Holly only shook her head, in a manner that suggested that there were lots of other meerkats she could have picked for a mate. Why did she pick me?

"And finally," she continued, after a long sigh, "A ramp will have to be constructed to allow the people, animals and supplies to be loaded up and through the top deck. It also needs to be 12 feet wide and 100 feet long to give us as low an angle to walk up and yet still be able to be stored safely on the top deck. When it comes time to hoist or lower it, we can have the elephants and some of the larger animals help them. We have to use a ramp; there is no way a hole cut into the side of this boat and then imagine we can keep it watertight. Maybe Noah got the word to make this floating refuge that way, but it just won't work. Not unless he just wants it to fill with water as the flood builds. It will never float unless we load everyone and everything from the top deck. [ed. note: See the accompanying

Appendix: "CUT-AWAY SKETCH OF NOAH'S ARK".]

"And to conclude for now, it may be helpful to give him and his family, and all the rest of us, some idea what the weight of this boat is going to be. By my quick estimations, broken down into the various compartments just described, the various weights would approximately be:

1. Keel and sundry add-ons throughout the boat- 1,160,000 pounds.
2. Bottom Deck and joists for other three decks- 1,600,000 pounds.
3. Sides, Bow and Stern- 450,000 pounds.
4. Deck planking for upper three decks- 55,800 pounds.

The total weight comes to 3,295,800 pounds or 1,478 displacement tons (no load). [ed. note: As far as I can tell, she based this estimate on the weight of one 4 inch by 4 inch by 10 foot treated beam being 21 pounds. For some comparisons, the U.S.S. Constitution had 2,200 displacement tons and the CVN Nimitz has 78,280 (no load) displacement tons.]

"One more thing before I forget. It might be beneficial to suggest to Noah that he consult with Nora. She, the other wives and children, who cannot help with cutting and shaping timber, need to begin gathering and collecting the stores for this trip. Again, by my rough estimate, there are going to have to be enough stores to last for approximately two years: one year for the flooding to occur and to dissipate and one year to allow plantings to grow enough to provide any food in the post-Flood world. I would suggest they begin making vast amounts of jerky. Otherwise, the carnivores amongst us are going to whittle down the final tally of people, animals and birds that finally get off this floating zoo. And the other thing is for them to make plenty of candles and oil lamps. They will be our only source of light inside the boat. Not everyone will have night vision, even if everyone wished they had.

"And that's it. Can you get this information to him right away?"

FIVE: "MERRILL, I THINK WE HAVE A PROBLEM!"

Well, as it turned out, I didn't get Holly's information to Noah right away. I got sick. It's one of my habits. If I get too excited, too nervous, too busy, too anything...I get a terrible head cold, along with headaches that are sometimes zingers. Just look at me. You can tell right away that my particular head size doesn't allow for extra large sinus cavity openings or for any unimpeded flow of air. Dust, dirt, heavy pollen, bad smells and head colds, or any unexpected excitement will clog them up for days, if not weeks. And while Holly, and a host of others around me, takes their infirmities in stride, I don't. I whimper and moan. I feel it's my duty to let others know that I'm uncomfortable; they could do the same if they wanted to. And Holly, bless her heart, puts up with it. But...not this time. After days of my moping, she told me to brace up and get outside. And, sure enough, it worked. I felt better immediately. Regardless, however, my feeling still is that a little hypochondria isn't such a bad thing; it brings out the strength of character in others.

So, four days after that first ark and flood-related meeting with Noah, as well as the same one in which Holly gave me her instructions, I scampered down our hillside to where there was obviously a lot of activity going on in a woodlot next to one of Noah's pastures. Unfortunately, I couldn't help but notice there was one potential problem with using that pasture; it also bordered the main road in and out of our valley, and connected the two towns on either side of it. It meant that townsfolk and country folk alike could easily view what was going on at Nora and Noah's place. And, as anyone knows, people talk. Maybe it's not as purposeful and truthful as what we animals say, but they do talk. And in this case, as in so many others, they also stirred up trouble. It's not that I wanted to appear jaded, but they would be seeing a lot of unusual activity. And to me, this project's visibility and proximity to the road could easily lead to problems.

And sure enough, by the time I got down to the pasture area, it was clear that a crowd was lined up along the roadside fence line, gawking at what Noah and his family were up to. I couldn't hear what they were saying, but it did appear that some of them were yelling, because they had their hands cupped around their mouths.

Once I got up beside Noah, who was a good six feet, four inches tall, and who was busy carrying on a serious conversation with Ham, who was also nearly as tall as Noah, I could tell they were having an intense conversation about something that was worrisome. Despite that, I began tapping on Noah's calf for attention. (One of my other more noticeable traits is that I'm not especially patient.) In response, he simply shifted his foot and leg, like he thought it was a midge or something else having a mid-morning snack inside his trousers. Again, I tapped. He stomped his foot. Finally, I pulled hard on his pants leg.

"Dang it, Ham, I've got something caught in my pants already this morning," he said as he looked down and saw me for the first time. "Well, Merrill, I see you finally decided to join us. What a surprise! I figured I had scared you off with our last conversation."

"Nope," I replied, "I was real sick."

But Noah and Holly both conversed frequently about most anything, and it was obvious that he already knew of my faux, health-related issues. So he just sighed and mumbled, "Ohh…"

"Well, anyway," I continued, feeling like what I had to say was more important than feeling pained that my maladies were a source of idle comment and dismissal, "I have some information for you, from Holly."

"And I've got another problem for you to deal with after you tell me what she has figured out," he quietly replied.

What followed, after that brief exchange, was both Ham and him sitting down on a couple of downed logs and letting me read from my notes that I had taken while Holly described the construction details for the boat. Throughout all my conversation, both men nodded frequently back and forth. It was obvious they were agreeing with what Holly had outlined to me. And after about an hour, I concluded my review; it was the first time they had a chance to take a deep breath.

"Nice presentation, Merrill," Noah exclaimed. "It's an ongoing fact; Holly never ceases to amaze me with her organizational skills. Why is it you don't have some of them as well?"

"I'm more the scribe type," I replied. "We're a team, Holly and I. She's the brains, and I'm the fingers who bring what she thinks and says to life."

"Well, it seems to work, God bless her. You always leave me a little lost as to what may happen after our conversations, but I always know once it gets into her hands, the final product will be just fine. Please thank her for me.

"But now we must discuss our next issue. There is a developing problem, becoming worse each day, with neighbors and strangers stopping by and wondering what we are doing here. I fear there are going to be repercussions if we don't set some parameters and have a cordon of security. I need you to slip over to the fence line by the road and listen for a while to what is being said. Then I need you to arrange some kind of protection for us and for this project. I worry things will get out of hand quickly if we aren't proactive from the start of this project.

"And while you're here, let me show you what we have done thus far. We started right away, after you suggested we begin falling trees and shaping them into cants afterward. As you can see, so far we have squared-off about thirty logs on three sides, as you advised. And from what you've just told me, we'll need to also find some larger trees to shape for the larger, keel stringers. We'll get on that right away, today."

"How many of you are working on this project?" I asked, quite amazed at what they had already accomplished.

"There are ten of us, divided equally into two, twelve-hour shifts. Shem, his three oldest boys and I work the daylight shift; and Ham, Japheth and their three sons work the night shift, which obviously is the much trickier one. They work by candle and moonlight, whenever that is possible. Fortunately, due to it entering its full-moon phase, we've had increased illumination the last two nights."

"I'm impressed," was all I could sincerely say. "Your dedication and commitment to this Command to build a boat of some sort is remarkable, but there is something I need to discuss with you before I embark on the two tasks you've assigned me."

"What's that?" Noah answered, rather impatiently.

"I'm glad to help you find some guards for the perimeter of this project, and assist them in developing a plan that doesn't create too much suspicion or ill-will throughout the region. And certainly, if you would also like me to, I'm willing to help spread the word out and about to have the various animals and birds choose who will be sailing on your boat, and even ask them to make the effort and take the time to collect the seeds from all the plant species that they either eat or just have in their individual neighborhoods and then bring them back here for you to store.

"But, as I mentioned a few days ago, I will not be mentioning to any of them the word 'clean' as a determining factor of how many are to be selected to board your boat. I realize there are observances, rites, customs and even sacrifices of some sort that you and your families practice; and I respect that. In all likelihood, these observances have helped keep you on a path that has been straighter and less tempting than the ones that others of your kind seem determined to follow. As we discussed previously, I will not be telling anyone that there will be 'seven' pair of some allowed, but only 'one' pair of others because some are clean and others aren't. That's just not the way it will work with me. I respect that you were commanded to do it that way, but you can notify the Floodmaster that your hired help is not cooperating and is plotting a revolt if that directive is insisted upon. And I take full responsibility for this objection and refusal. I cannot, in good faith, speak to my fellow animals and birds about such a potentially catastrophic upcoming event and have this exclusion clause hanging over me.

"To put a fine point on this thorny issue, my proposal is that everyone is to be told to pick a pair of their kind to show up at a prearranged time, which for some may be quite soon. For example, you will probably need some of these larger animals right away to guard the perimeter; to help lift, shove and hold timbers in place; and to move downed trees into a designated area.

"But, as well and in addition, I will also tell each species that they can pick up to six other pairs as alternates to come as well. They will be told there is no guarantee that any of them will accompany you. And yet, my guess is that the smaller of this vast company will be allowed to have more pairs come aboard, as well as those that you routinely use for your own nourishment, for instance, their milk, eggs, wool and cheese.

"Under no circumstance will I mention using of any of them, whether it is a young or a mature animal or bird for food, sacrifice, to make some clothing or eventually to fashion for leather. I can appreciate the manner in which you use such items for your own survival, but if you hope to get the broadest scope in number of animals and birds to go along with taking this voyage of yours, you have to guarantee me, and them, that nothing of that nature will occur to them or to their offspring. If the animal is aged or ill, then that could be a matter for discussion and arbitration.

"Also, I need to add that you'll need to take along a large amount of molasses or syrup to feed your hives of honey bees. That will be their only source of food during your boat trip; and you'll need all of them for pollinating your fruit and nut trees, along with the many vegetables you plant, once you get settled.

"So, there are my terms. Will you agree to them?"

"For being a rather scatter-brained, deeply

burrowing and overly nervous critter, you make a convincing challenge and argument. And I concede the use of the word 'clean' is prejudicial. It's like saying the 'best', the 'purest' or the 'whitest'. That being the case, I will offer up your comments in my prayers tonight, and if there is some major objection, I'll let you know. Otherwise, go ahead with your plan. It won't be easy, no matter how you phrase it, to convince the wildlife kingdom out there to give it all up and follow you here. You will now become like a shepherd. And they must trust you to be such. And I will tentatively agree with your conditions, as you've outlined them. Now see what you can do about those folks gawking at us over at that fence line."

Both my outburst and my being designated as the project's "shepherd" came as a complete surprise to me. Holly always told me I was too shy and withdrawn about my views and opinions. I couldn't wait till I told her what I said that day! I knew she'd either be proud of me or aghast. And next, I was facing the impossibly daunting job of trying to understand and cope with people. Give me strength!

It didn't take me more than a few minutes to slink my way around the woodlot and, without being noticed, position myself close to the fence line, where a number of bystanders were already collecting to watch what Noah and his family were up to. In my half-hidden position, I hunkered down and watched and listened.

It wasn't too long after I had done this that Holly shared with me her accumulated-over-the-

course-of-time impressions of people. To her, there always appeared to be three types of human beings. The first, and luckily the smallest type, were those who maybe once compassionately tried to observe people and events around them, but they developed a sighted blindness. Early on in this transformation, they became filled with overwhelmingly violent and preconceived prejudices, biases and hatreds; and seeing anything else but themselves was impossible. Their field of vision was filled with hate and malice; it filled their horizons. Who were they? Too often, they seemed to be the so-called leaders of the people who lived around us, and it seemed to her that they squeezed the very life out of those around them.

And those, who this first group terrorized and ruled, could be divided into the last two types of humans. The largest are those who visualize things around them with a sharp, unblinking focus. They stare intensely through a narrow corridor that is immediately ahead of them. Because of this, they are often quite talented and skilled in a particular activity. For instance, it could be in woodworking, pottery making and painting, sculpturing or voicing their views on a limited range of subjects. They were, for the most part, the more highly sought after members of any village. But they occasionally seemed to drift into the outer fringes of the above, unseeing group, if their views become too rigid. Further, Holly added, she noticed that they were the ones who more often became lost in the woods, due to their focusing so hard on one given area and ignoring the wider world around them.

The last types of humans that she described were those who scan the world around them. She noted that they looked about themselves with softer eyes, not focusing so unflinchingly hard on one thing in particular. And interestingly, she also observed that they didn't get lost as easily in our nearby woods and surrounding wilderness areas. They were more capable of seeing trends develop, and were more likely to remain continually open to options that others dismissed as impractical. Most often, they seemed to engage in vocations such as building, designing and of thinking about and creating new avenues of opportunity. They were more at ease accepting new ideas, making changes or devising unique approaches to see the so-called mundane. They appeared to Holly to be more open to discovery and exploration, of adapting to new or evolving situations. But there were fewer of these folks about, at least in our region, she noted. They seemed to threaten the other two categories and find themselves often the source of persecution and marginalization.

Even now, as I recall her telling me all this, I marvel at her ability to study the world around us, to synthesize it into an understandable outline and then to grace me, of all creatures, with an explanation of what she observes. The best I could ever do was to find some food for our next meal. She is a marvel.

And frankly, as I huddled by that fence line the remaining portion of that day, the conversations I overheard were not conducted by people in Holly's third category. It was worrisome. There was a growing concern building among the bystanders. They were confused and couldn't understand what was happening. It was not part of an ordinary day; it was out of their focus. And I sensed their confusion could easily turn into their feeling threatened with something new and unexplainable.

More worrisome still was my concern that violence might erupt; something that I've noticed was so often the method of choice for people dealing with their confusion and any different or new ideas, developments or events.

Noah was right. I needed to gather together a band of cohorts to protect and defend what he and his family were doing. But first I needed to let Holly know how my conversation with Noah went, and what I had observed and been told to do.

SELECTION AND PREPARATION

SIX: THE GUARDIANS

Well, to be honest with you, the conversation that evening with Holly did not go as I expected. Of course, bear in mind that for me, rarely anything does. My capacity to imagine, understand or anticipate reactions or events should require me finding something that says, "See instruction booklet before opening or discussing anything". I didn't come equipped with the skills others have to cope with and maneuver through daily life. Up until these encounters with Noah, I took each day as it came, tried to do whatever my DNA coding preordained, protected Holly the best I knew how, and kept whatever food I could rustle up on the table. But then my world began to unravel, as it appeared it soon would for every plant, animal and person on this planet. And Holly was about to stunningly bring this fact stunningly home to me.

She reacted to my telling her about the inquisitive and possibly disruptive look-e-loo's at the pasture's fence line, and to the reality of Noah building an ark remarkably based on the outline she dictated to me, with panic and horror.

"Merrill," she cried out, after being silent the entire time I recounted what I saw and did for the day, "all this is just terrible. Even if it's true that what Noah says is going to happen...does happen; who is going to believe you? Look at you! You're no heavenly spirit. I love you dearly, but let's face it, you and I both know this is not a challenge you're equipped to meet. You quite adequately fulfill the responsibilities which are delegated to you; and you are diligent in preparing for our hoped-for, future family. But notifying the animal and bird kingdom of their ultimate demise...you? No way!"

Now, let me be honest here. That did hurt a little bit. It was true, of course. Holly was never off the mark by much, with anything she did or said. But I had taken Noah's directives for me as some kind of recognition and confidence that I was "the man". So, while I didn't argue with Holly (it never worked), I did voice some minor-key groans and grunts to indicate my disagreement with her.

"Face it, Merrill," she went on, "there is probably nothing going to happen with all this. Noah will cut down a bunch of trees, shape a few of them and then call it quits. It will ultimately serve the purpose of a little more land clearing for extending his pasture. Furthermore, his sons and grandchildren will soon tire of all this silliness and walk off the job. It's doomed to failure, because it's too preposterous a notion. And now you and I have been drawn into it. This involvement of yours must stop NOW!!"

"But, Holly," I mumbled, feeling thoroughly chastised, "Noah did seem to have had some really authentic and authoritative orders issued to him. And you've got to admit, he and his family aren't like the other folks who we see and can't help but worry about. He and his family, as we've noticed, appear to be special in some way. Everybody else who we encounter appears angry or manipulative; they seem preoccupied with cheating, robbing, taking life for granted or taking it from others. Things are a mess, I've got to admit, and I know you've seen it too."

"That may be," she replied, "but why do all the animals, birds and plants have to suffer because of it? Answer me that!"

"I haven't the slightest idea," I moaned out loud. "Maybe it's only by wiping the slate clean that the world can start anew and be the place where everyone gets along, doesn't hurt one another and respects the lives and habitat of each of us. It's pretty clear that the way it's going right now, there isn't going to be any of this left in the years ahead. Maybe it is a sacrifice that is necessary to make amends for everything that has gone wrong."

"But what wrong have we or our extended family done?" came the quick response. "Or what transgression was so severe that the birds that fly in and out of here must all perish? Why can't there just be a plague, or a more finely targeted catastrophe that befalls the people alone? Let them disappear, not the likes of us! It's just not right, nor

46

is it fair!!"

"Honestly, I agree," was all I could say. "But I think there is something so serious afoot, so sternly ordered, in such an unmistakable manner that Noah could do nothing less than respond as he has. And in talking to him, you can tell he is fully committed, as is his family. Maybe it might help if you go down yourself and talk to him. I'm sure he would appreciate seeing and talking to you. He highly respects you and your advice.

"In the meantime, I must go on with what he has instructed me to do. To be honest, I don't have any logical reason for doing so. I'm acting on trust, following orders regarding something that someone else has been told to do. True enough, it has all come to me second hand. That means you, I and everyone one that we talk to will have to do the same. For all of us, there will be trickle-down announcements and directives for this upcoming Event.

"What was immediate, wondrous, mystifying, holy and uncontestable for the individual who was first informed and instructed to do all this, will now be something we have to accept on faith as true and try to become faithful followers. My sense right now is that this initial encounter of Noah's is the beginning of some kind of pattern that will not stop with this first, terrifying news. It may be the shape of things to come. Someone special experiences a miracle or gets frightfully stunning orders, and the rest of us, upon getting this same news second or third hand, try to become faithful believers. It's picking and choosing the truthfulness of that first spokesperson that will be the tricky part. And for me I feel that Noah is truthful."

"Ok, then, this is what I am going to do," Holly grudgingly answered, "I will see that you are as prepared as possible to undertake your mission, BUT I will be marching down to Noah's place and talking to both him and Nora as soon as you leave here. My heart is broken over the implication of all that you've told me and the way things are progressing. And I don't think you should get your hopes up that whoever you tell is going to accept it any easier than I have. Why should they? My guess is that when the day comes that the rain is supposed to start, if it ever does, you and Noah will be standing there at the loading ramp with no one but yourselves waiting to board your mammoth, floating, log hotel. The only thing this entire affair may be good for afterward is that he and you will have a huge roadside attraction, a novelty boat that never floated or sailed. And that is all I am going to say about this now.

"I guess next, we have to get you ready. Did he say anything further to you about how you are to accomplish your impossible tasks?"

"As a matter of fact, he did," I remembered. "He said I was to be his 'shepherd'."

"I wouldn't say that is too great a help. It seems to me you're going to be a lot more than that."

"Like what?" I asked, taken aback that even more was going to be expected of me.

"Well, the way I see it, you're first going to be the wailer of warnings, then the dispatcher of despair, followed up with being the coordinator of the convinced and finally, maybe the shepherd of the stranded. And you'll be doing all this with the oddest and largest assortment of animal and bird life that was ever assembled and corralled in a given space.

"And look at you! Even as much as I love you, I would probably hesitate to follow you inside a sumptuous banquet hall, filled with mounds of eatables and treats, much less allow you to lead me into a huge, log box that is supposed to mount up and float away in a world-convulsing flood. You've got to change your appearance to meet and inform the public of what's ahead. You need to improve it by having the look of authority."

"How?" I inquired, now thinking all this was going too far.

"Take me as I am", I thought. Let the message do all the impressing, not the messenger. I was just its mouthpiece. Who will care how I look? But then, I remembered that it was Holly who had much more experience interacting with the public. And she reminded me daily that appearances mean everything today. What you wear, how you speak, how well you are groomed, your diction and your manners, these are the criteria that determine the size of audience that will listen to you. It is not simply your message, that's for sure. Consequently, no one ever paid any attention to me until Noah did five days ago. And that's probably because he doesn't mix much with the John Q. Public either.

So reluctantly, I squared my shoulders and repeated, "How?"

"First off, you're going to have to take a real bath… using water. No more of those famous dirt baths of yours. You'll head down to our nearby stream, take a bar of soap and scrub yourself thoroughly. Then when you get back here, I'll need to groom you with a good deal of barbering, nit picking and combing you down, from head to toe. You've got tangles everywhere. I never say anything, but I wonder sometimes what you must be hiding in all that matted hair net of yours. Next, you'll have to brush and floss your teeth, followed by a thorough gargle of some rose water. Your almost exclusive diet of scorpions hasn't done much for your breath being socially acceptable. So often I've noticed what appears to be a stinger dangling out the side of your mouth and wanted to say something. But I didn't want to hurt your feelings.

"And then finally, we have to decide on something for you to carry, a symbol that will signal to everyone that you are coming into their midst with a special and urgent message. It will have to be something so startling that it will immediately get their attention, but not so threatening that they will become defensive and hostile. After all, you are going to be speaking to perfect strangers, many of whom probably wouldn't mind having you for lunch. You need to gently distract them from those urges, and then proceed immediately with your message.

"And your mentioning that Noah called you 'his shepherd' gives me an idea. Why don't you carry a sheep-herder's staff with you? We'll attach it to a belt around your waist when you are hurrying along to your next convocation; and then once you arrive there, you can stand tall, holding it at your side. It will symbolize that your intent is meant to shelter and lead, not threaten nor harm. I think I can fashion one myself before you leave later today. I'll set about making one while you are down taking a bath.

"Last, but certainly not a minor nor an insignificant least, have you given any thought as to how you are going to accomplish the three objectives that Noah has outlined for you? I'm almost surprised he didn't ask you to build the boat as well."

Finally, I had a chance to speak, but my throat and mouth had turned to chalk, listening to all she had listed for me to do. I was spellbound. But, attempting to show that I was mustering up some courage and will power to meet these challenges, I said, "Yes, I have."

"I envision," I began, "dividing his requests amongst three, distinct groups of animals and birds. One group will involve my speaking with certain migrating birds, the ones who will carry Noah's message to the furthest corners of the world. Another will be the ones who will provide the protection at his building site. And the last one will be with the individuals who will be formed into committees that will coordinate and oversee all the various stages of this entire building process and the upcoming voyage.

"Without a doubt, the most urgent, and probably the riskiest, is the group I need to organize for protecting Noah's farm; I'm going to call them the 'Guardians'. They will have to be told why he is building a boat and then be asked to protect him and his family, at least initially. But later on they will have to protect all of us who assemble there and eventually board the boat before it floats off. And you're right, it will take a lot of convincing to get anyone to agree to do any of this.

"First, however, I need to follow up on what you've suggested...in the clearest of terms. I'll immediately go down to our stream and take a long, cold bath, and then you can do my 'make over'. I'll be back looking like a new 'kat'; you'll see."

And sure enough just like she promised, while I was gone she rustled up some crooked tree branch from an Ebony tree, then polished and shaped it into a perfectly formed and curved shepherd's staff. Holly told me she wanted it to be brightly colored black, so as to contrast loudly with my brownish-tan coat. In addition, she made it long enough to fit comfortably over my shoulder when I was standing or walking, which I rarely did, unless it was a formal occasion. She said it was my symbol of authority; but the curved lines signaled that it was not intended to hurt anyone nor was it to be seen as a weapon. And, believe it or not, it worked. No stranger I ever approached carrying it bristled or challenged me. And along with it, once she had me combed, dusted, flossed and deodorized, I looked and felt ready to spread Noah's instructions throughout the land. Or at least I did for the first twenty paces after I left our home.

I've found that self-confidence is one of those most fleeting of my emotions. One glance, gesture or word from anyone will turn me into a melted marshmallow. I become Mr. Gooey Guts. And upon taking my twenty-first step away from Holly and our home, that same old feeling began to creep over me.

Sensing that was happening to me, Holly cried out, as I passed further down the eastern side of our hillside home, heading toward the Okavango Delta region, "Be strong! Have courage, Merrill! You can do this. It's not just Noah who needs you to make this happen; it's all of us. And know I love you…"

*It was just the reinforcement I needed at that moment to bolster my confidence and to provide me with the necessary support for what lay ahead. Maybe there was some **Higher Authority**, **All Seeing Presence** or even some **Master Conductor**, a **Floodmaestro**, overseeing all these preparations and then initiating The Flood; **One** who Holly and I were supposed to follow and **Who** would be strengthening and blessing us. But I had no lingering doubts or hesitancy about her importance in my life when she called out to me. I felt infused with a determination, which overcame my total awkwardness and fear of what I was about to do.*

After she shouted at me, I turned and waved my staff back at her and then picked up my pace, hurrying forward into the forests and marshes of the Delta, where all manner of animal life lived…and hunted.

It was probably an hour into my struggling through the undergrowth, which became thicker and thicker as I approached the first of many river tributaries, that I came upon the two individuals that I most wanted to find first. They were to be my choice of who would supervise and coordinate the Guardians. They were Lewis and Lois, my two lion friends.

I spied them resting next to a huge banyan tree. [ed. note: Bear in mind at the time of this chronicle, the Earth had only one, super continent; it was called "Pangaea". It was to eventually separate and become the five distinct continents that we know today. Nora, Noah, Holly and Merrill lived in what became Africa, with what later became known as India on its eastern border and North and South America on its western border.] The day had become too hot for hunting, and Lewis was dozing as I approached them. Lois cocked her head when she saw me. I think it was my black shepherd's staff that caught her eye first.

"What's up, Merrill?" she called out. "And what's with the black stick? You got a gimpy leg or something? If so, it looks to me like it's a little too long for a crutch. Bring it over and I'll crunch it down to size for you."

"Nope," I replied. "It's not a crutch. It's my shepherd's stave."

"What's a shepherd, Merrill?"

"I'm not too sure… to be perfectly honest. But I think it's supposed to be someone who helps others."

"Do we need help, Merrill? Lewis, and I here, feel pretty content right about now, and I can't think of any help that we need. You're not trying to sell something again, are you? I remember the last time we saw you, you were peddling some kind of mouthwash and shampoo kit."

"No, no. I'm not here for anything like that. I'm here to ask your help. But before I do, I need to tell you and Lewis something of the gravest importance.

"What could that be?"

"It's like this," I began. "Noah, you know…the fellow who lives on the other side of that range of hills to the west of here, has just given me some detailed information and instructions, and you are the first ones to hear it… besides Holly, who I'm sure you remember."

"Oh, yeah," Lois replied. "We well remember Holly. She's the really smart one."

"That's her," I said proudly. And upon her saying that, Lewis yawned, opening his sprawling mouth, exposing the longest and most teeth I had ever seen in any one place. It was all I could do to not start running back home and forgetting this entire matter. But Lewis then spoke and restored my fleeting sense of self-confidence.

"Hey, there Merrill," Lewis roared after he'd just taken in a great breath. "How's it hanging, old man? Lois and I were just talking about you and Holly the other day… just after we'd had a big lunch. Isn't that right, hon?"

Lois simply nodded, as she eyed me, as if sizing me up for which course they were thinking of next that afternoon. But I didn't jokingly blurt out that we were probably being considered for dessert.

"What brings you back into our neighborhood?" he asked, somewhat impatiently.

Clearing my throat, I began, "Well, you see, Lewis, it was like I was about to tell Lois, here. Noah Schwartz, over the way, has recently given me some really awful news and then asked me to pass it along. He also asked me to look into providing a secure perimeter around their farm for him and his family for the next few months." And after announcing that, I proceeded to tell them the entire story of Noah's conversations with me, what he and his family were building and what specifically I needed the two of them to do.

"Are you telling us," Lewis began, after I'd finished my monologue, "that there is going to be a storm that is going to last so long that everything, everywhere, is going to be under water? And that you have to arrange to have representatives of all the animals, birds and plants that roam or grow on this planet to show up to sail on this ship of bad dreams? You've got to be completely out of your mind!! How are we supposed to believe you? And why are we supposed to guard these crazy boat-builders, particularly if they are the ones who are going to leave us behind?"

My response to his understandable outburst was halted and filled with self-doubt, but I had to push forward. Something was driving me now to pursue this task with all the energy that was in me.

"I asked Noah these same questions," I began. "Holly and I, she more than me, had the same reaction. It seems Noah was so convinced by the tone and force of the **Floodmaster's** voice and presence that it left no doubt as to the veracity of what he was hearing. And because we both know that Noah and his family are not like the other people we see and hear about, I eventually had to accept his word. Plus, you should go over for yourselves and see the work that he and his sons and their children are doing. They, too, believed him. Just go over there. No strings attached.

And if you don't agree once you get there, then just turn around, come back here and forget the whole thing. Pretend I never told you anything. It won't take you more than a half day to do it. If fact, I'll wait here while you go over. Speak to Noah while you're at it. And see for yourself what I'm saying about the growing numbers of people who are congregating at his fence line. It's a potentially explosive situation. He needs your help. And you can pick whoever you need to help you. Just see for yourselves. Please. Go ahead.

"Then, when you get back here, if you are convinced, we can discuss any further details. One thing I might add, if you agree to at least go see for yourselves, and if you agree to be involved in this undertaking, I'm sure you will be one of the pairs of selected occupants for his upcoming boat trip. And that would be the case for anyone else who you decided needed to help you protect Noah and his family. It might help you with your own recruitment to know that. Plus, you should tell anyone you ask to bring some food and provisions along with them. More will be provided, and you could take turns getting more during your period of protecting the Schwartz's, but I'd start stockpiling foodstuffs right away.

"And one final thing. I will need to speak

with one other couple about becoming members of your self-selected troop. I would like to add them to your short list of possible recruits."

"Who might they be?" Lois sighed.

"Elliot and Elaine," I answered.

"The two elephants who live down the road a piece?"

"Yes, those nice folks," I replied. "I'd like them to be a part of your protective contingent at Noah's, should you decide to do this.

Looking at one another, and mumbling something that I couldn't understand, it was Lois who finally turned to me and said, "Ok, we'll head over to Noah's place now. We don't have anything else on our schedule for the day, lucky for you. And we'll plan on meeting you back here around sunset. We'll give you our answer then."

Relieved, I agreed and watched them both stand up, stretch, yawn again and then begin a fast-paced trot off in the direction I just came from. Exhausted from all the emotion, discussions and sleepless nights I'd been having since Noah first mentioned all this to me; I curled up, with my staff resting beside me, and slept dreamlessly until they returned.

So soundly did I sleep that it didn't seem like any time passed before I was awakened by one of Lois's front paws shaking me awake.

"Wake up, Merrill. We're back," Lois called out, somewhat breathless. "And we met and spoke with your Noah fellow. Nice guy and a nice family, if I do say so. And we saw what they are trying to build, the plans that Holly outlined for them and the crowds of people shuffling to and fro along their property. And you're right about everything."

"Do you believe me then, about the upcoming flood?" I hurriedly interrupted.

"Maybe not entirely, and I suspect deep down, neither do you. But, on our return trip, Lewis and I agreed that Noah and his family members who took time to speak with us were sincere and dedicated enough to their tasks that we decided there must be something to it. You can't have that many people agreeing wholeheartedly about something very often, particularly if they are all in the same family. That counts for something. And we certainly agree with you about the growing crowds. They could easily become unruly and cause lots of trouble for those hard working folks.

"So?" I insisted.

"So, yes, we'll help you. And if worse comes to worse, we'll hop on that boat, if the rains start and if it is ever finished enough to stay afloat."

"Did Noah or Nora say anything specific you might need to do or prepare before you return, if you did decide to join them?" I followed up, feeling overjoyed that my first recruiting effort was a success.

"Yes, Nora did. She said we should probably begin looking for food supplies that could be added to their stockpile for the trip. She showed us the dried fruit and jerky they were preparing. And she emphasized that there would not be much of that on board for us to gorge ourselves on. Amazingly, she advised us that we might seriously consider our diet becoming more vegetarian in content. Can you believe that! Us? The kings of the jungle, pampas, forest and local neighborhoods becoming Vegans!!? I can just see Lewis munching down on a plate full of bean sprouts or me tossing in a mouth full of pine nuts. It left us speechless. But as we worked our way back here, we decided it made a certain amount of sense. So, we'll even give that a try.

"But mind you, Merrill, if all this turns out to be a silly venture or some kind of touristy, jive amusement park, you'll be tops on our menu for hors d'oeuvres immediately thereafter. In the meantime, we are going to prepare to head back over there."

"Before you do, there is one other thing you need to do," I interrupted, trying to change the subject of me being some kind of pre-meal, tasty treat.

"What's that?"

"You and Lewis need to make a list and contact the other members of your team, the ones you want to assist you as Guardians," I replied.

"Oh, we've already considered that and plan to get right on it tomorrow morning at first light," she replied.

"Could I ask who you are considering?"

"It's pretty straightforward," Lewis chimed in, having sat down beside Lois and having another one of his frightful yawns. "We're going to round up the biggest and/or the meanest in the neighborhood. We've decided on recruiting a pair each of tigers, elephants, Cape buffaloes, rhinoceroses, hippopotamuses, lynxes, and chimpanzees. But chances are we'll ask for more than just two chimpanzees; they'll be our scouts and work the surrounding forests better than the others of us. And we hope to have them all in place at Noah's by the end of this week."

I was breathless after hearing all this. It was actually happening. Holly's boat was being built. Lewis and Lois were on board, so to speak, along with their commitment to help and enlist others. I was so relieved. However, there was one modification I had to make to their plan.

"Fine folks," I began, "I need to ask one small favor before you set off on your recruitment tour tomorrow morning."

"Now what?" Lewis boomed.

"No, no, it's nothing more for you to do," I quickly replied. "It's just that I need you to direct me to where I might locate Elaine and Elliot."

Looking at each other, the two lions laughed and gave a sigh of relief. "Of course we can. They are, actually, old friends of ours. And we'd love to have them along to help. Tell them that they will probably have multiple jobs, particularly if they can convince a few of their cousins to help out as well. We're sure Noah could use their extra muscle in moving and lifting those logs. And tell them we told you this."

Relieved that we were of one mind, I decided it was time for me to move on before it became too dark for me to navigate these woods safely. Our goodbyes were short and to the point. By then, we were each beginning to realize the full impact of what we were agreeing to and why. This was not a time to celebrate or to congratulate one another. Something horrible was going to happen in the near future. And we each knew, deep down, that our being forewarned made us vulnerable to despair and possible harm.

It's funny, in an odd sort of way. A sense of doom, whether it's fostered by a change in the weather, from foreign aggression, economic collapse or social upheaval, precedes the actual event. If you are fully aware of your surroundings, monitoring the behavior of those around you or observing the sky above or the earth beneath you, there are definite signs of collapse, ahead of the actual event. We miss the signals when we become entrapped by distracting obsessions, such as accumulating money, possessions, converts, property or other inhabitants of this world. Those of us chosen by Noah were to become more and more aware of this sense of impending peril. An end was coming. And more frightening to each of us was the haunting question: was there to be a new beginning?

Shaking off my reverie, I bid Lois and Lewis good-by and hurried off, hoping to locate my two elephant friends as soon as possible. Luckily, I did. And they were only about five miles further away, toward the east. The conversation with them paralleled the one I had with Lois and Lewis, and they, too, decided to go see Noah in the morning and size up the situation. By noon that next day they were back to where I was waiting for them, and again, they both agreed to help. In addition, they were certain they could get some help from their relatives for Noah. It was uncomfortable for me to advise them that the additional family members probably would not be part of the contingent that eventually would be allowed on board the finished boat, even though they helped to build it. It was agreed, that fact would be presented to them beforehand, and then let them decide if they want to do it anyway.

By the end of my sixth day since Noah had first informed me of this pending flood, the process of selection was well underway. But each step from here on would become more difficult, and a backlash was building, unbeknownst to Noah or me.

SEVEN: THE MESSENGERS

The next morning I set off, leaving Elliot and Elaine fast asleep. I supposed their journey the day before was exhausting and that they would probably sleep all day. But I had many miles to cover before I would reach my destination. In fact, I expected I would have to walk at least two full days to reach the Okavango River, and then another day or two before I came to the Delta region.

And sure enough, it wasn't until dusk the second day that I found myself at the shoreline of the river. And what a magnificent river it was! Some say it's the clearest, most pristine water in the world. I couldn't go out into the rapid-flowing current, but from whatever vantage point I looked down into it, I could always see the river bed just as clear as if there wasn't twenty to thirty feet of water above it.

I suspected that it was because of its clarity and lack of pollutants that birdlife the world over came to its tributaries and the Delta each year to hatch and rear their young. Not having been here before, I still had been told by the passing flocks stopping by our home that this was the place to come if you wanted to see every imaginable bird in existence in one place. And that is exactly what I wanted to do. Or at least to make contact with the ones that migrated back and forth to the furthest reaches of land everywhere, in all directions.

As an aside, in case anyone wonders who might read this later, we, and by "we", I mean everyone - people, animals and birds - all speak the same language. There is some limitation on how far down the food chain, if you pardon the expression, that speech is possible. Usually anything smaller than three inches in length doesn't talk, nor do fish, at least that's to the best of my knowledge.

Actually, that is a stroke of good fortune for me and Holly, because I'm not sure I could eat anything that talked as I was doing so. Scorpions, my tastiest treat, can't, and even if they did, I doubt it would be anything socially acceptable. They always appear to me to have such a bad disposition. On the other hand, there are the lions and some of the larger animals that do dine on those (or we) who speak. As gruesome as it sounds, however, I know they try to pick on those who are infirm or aged. It's a survival thing. Still, it turns my blood cold to think about it.

Just the same, then there are people. They speak. They even speak the same language that we all do; but so many of them seem to thrill in killing each other, and any of us other folk who might get in their way. Again, what's that all about? I bet if they always had to eat what they killed, they wouldn't have this seemingly wanton desire. It's one that Holly and I have often observed. And you'd even think their speaking the same language would eliminate the need to be so disagreeable. I can't imagine what carnage there would be if humans spoke different languages; or if we couldn't speak, to at least rationally argue our case before they turned their madness loose on us.

[ed note: Apparently, no animals or birds born after The Flood had the ability to speak. And what, in particular, has remained so unusual, even insulting if you will, about the record and stories surrounding that most-famous voyage and its passengers, was that we never had the opportunity, until now, to finally tell our side of this story. As I just recently learned myself, our ability wasn't something that Noah was especially eager to pass along, when he began churning out the press reports on this Event. And as things unraveled after that Flood, I guess the Folks in charge of that Deluge and what came afterward, were also not anxious to confuse the situation with all of us having our say or even having the ability again. Supposedly, the hope was that if the ability to talk was limited to just humans, then the problems necessitating The Flood in the first place would be avoided in the future. Now, there was a colossal mistake for you. It looks to me that given the present state of things, you folks desperately need all the advice you can get!]

And it was while I was gazing from a lofty viewpoint out over the river that a passing loon happened to land beside me, somewhat out of breath. Startled, I turned to it and asked, "Are you ok?"

"Yeah... sort of... maybe, well... not entirely," he stammered in reply. "That last leg of this journey back here is always a killer. And I had to kick it into high gear to make the last hundred miles or so. But, actually, that wasn't the worst of it. To be honest, I'm terrified, more than I've ever been in my life. So do you mind if I just rest here a while?"

"Be my guest," I politely offered, extending a paw in a swooping motion. "What, if I may ask, has scared you so? Were you nearly attacked by a hawk or something else on the way here? Or are you lost and unsure what to do next?"

"None of that," he hurriedly answered, still panting. "And it's hard to explain. Something awful appears nearly ready to happen! You can just sense it all around; at least you could where I just came from."

"Where was that?!" I interjected, now feeling myself tensing and becoming more alarmed.

"From the edge of land, from where 'The Stretch', as most of us call it, begins."

"What do you mean by 'The Stretch'"?

"It's what appears to be an endless body of water, stretching out as far as you can see, even when we are high aloft circling to migrate back here or elsewhere. And from what I am told, this same terrifying phenomenon exists everywhere around the land you are standing on. Just in case you didn't know it, you are standing on one mammoth piece of ground that extends in all directions for thousands of miles. BUT surrounding it is this water that never ends, as far as anyone knows. No one I know has ever been able to fly out and reach land on the other side. It seems to go on forever.

"And in the past there have been storms that come and go, which do seem to originate from that direction, at least whenever I've been living in that distant region, far to the north of here. However, what I've just witnessed, something that began about two weeks ago is far different from a casual thunderstorm or gale."

"How so?" I asked, becoming even more nervous at his description and knowing what I already did from Noah's prediction.

"It began its formation pretty much as any other cloudy day, as far as I recall. And yet it was not the same. For days it continued to gather more clouds, as if sucking up more and more moisture from 'The Stretch'. And while doing so, it got darker and darker. And it began to rumble as if coming from deep down in someone's chest. Gradually, the volume began to build into a roar that seemed to be everywhere. And by the time I fled the area, it was a screaming howl, with total blackness extending up higher than any clouds I've ever seen before. There seemed to be no end of them, as I looked skyward. Saying all this, none of what I've described is what has me nearly paralyzed with fear."

"Then, what does?" I asked, not sure I wanted to hear his answer.

"It was that this storm front didn't come on shore. In the week I was there watching it form, it never made landfall. It simply came to the shoreline and screamed louder and louder. And in talking to my migrating companions on the way down here over these last few days, they have seen the same thing everywhere else as well. It's as if this gigantic storm is paused to come on shore, just waiting for a signal, and then it will pounce on all of us at once."

Hearing this last bit of his story gave me goose-bumps. It began to shake my self-confidence that I could complete the jobs that Noah had given me. I knew right away there had to be a connection between what Lance, this loon fellow, whose name I learned somewhat later, was telling me and Noah's description of what was about to occur. I felt that dread was about to paralyze me. I could just envision what was ahead for us all. It was a nerve-racking few moments of complete silence that followed Lance's revelations. Finally I spoke.

"There is something I need to tell you," I began. "But first I'd like to know your name and whether you have anyone accompanying you here."

And after our formal introductions and finding out that his lifetime partner should be flying in any minute, I proceeded to tell him all that I had told the pair of lions and elephants. Midway during the course of my briefing his mate, Lolly, flew in and landed beside him. Immediately, she became engrossed in what I was saying, even without having to repeat myself. She immediately reminded me of Holly; bright, quick and patient with her fumbling spouse. I felt I eased their fears somewhat by the end of my statement when I suggested that they could join the ones who would travel on Noah's boat. But honestly, it was clear that they had been given too much information to absorb fully in such a short time. In fact, they were speechless for some time following my report.

Finally, as a signal that Lance was recovering somewhat from the shock of all he'd witnessed and just heard, he asked, "Where's this boat being built? Lolly and I will probably fly over that way as soon as we get our wind back, and then we'll let you know what we think about your invitation."

"Is there someone else we can talk with to confirm what you have just told us?" Lolly then asked.

I suggested they stop by our burrow on the way back here and call in on Holly. By this time I was sure she, too, would have spoken with Noah and would have been convinced that what he was telling me was probably truthful. They both nodded in agreement with that plan.

Then Lance followed up with, "What's with the curved pole? Are you also one of those diviners who 'witches' for water? If so, you found the mother lode here. Just look at that mighty and magnificently clear river!"

"It's my shepherd's staff," I replied with some élan.

"That's odd," came his response to both my answer and the associated, self-satisfied smugness. You sure don't look like any shepherd I ever saw. And from the looks of things as I flew in here, your sheep must have all made a run for it. You'd better change jobs or your stick's description. But then,

70

again, maybe on second thought, it's folks like us that are now going to be your sheep." And saying that, both of them soared off, heading west toward Noah's.

Extending my staff to stop them just prior to their flying off to meet with Noah and Holly, I suggested that we meet at the point where the Okavango River divided into its countless smaller rivers and streamlets, forming the Delta. As I had heard it described to me, it's a place where the Okavango resembles a kind of broom handle and its myriad tributaries become its bristles, which serve to sweep the region with life-giving and life-sustaining water. [ed. note: As you are probably aware, this river, with its dozens of off-springs, still exists. They form a vast, lush network each rainy season for the most diverse population of African animals and birds anywhere on the continent. But if you weren't aware, you are now.]

Further, I requested that, provided they were convinced by talking to Holly and Noah about what I had told them, and if that confirmed their darkening suspicions of what they had seen and heard along the seashore, they should seek out and recruit six other pairs of loons, and seven pairs each of terns, gulls, geese, ducks, swans, cranes, storks, eagles, hawks and ospreys. They were to tell them to meet me at the highest point, near where the Okavango made its first division into its tributaries. This location was about a two days' walk for me from our present location. And I would be on the west side of the river, as I presently was at that time. There was no way I could navigate across the river or find my way through that Delta, brimming with thick jungle canopies, marshes and swamps.

Besides, I belonged on dry land. I only get wet whenever Holly insists I take a bath. Rivers make me nervous, as does any water. And wouldn't you know, Noah picked me for this job. He and that Flood of his; I was no match for either. I was beginning to feel very underqualified and poorly suited for his tasks.

But, anyway, it wasn't long after their departure that I decided to resume my walk. I had committed myself to reaching the Delta assembly area before them and my choice of specific, world-migrating birds that I needed. This area was likewise the wintering-over location for all the Earth's migratory birds. [ed. note: Picture in your mind millions upon millions of actual "snowbirds" congregating at one place... like Quartzsite, Arizona.] Along the way, I needed to compose myself for what decisions still lay ahead and to devise a plan on how best to have The Warning and accompanying Invitation delivered by the Messengers.

The next two days of travel passed uneventfully. I was able to stay on an outcrop of hills, overlooking the river all the way to the point where I could gaze out and see it fanning out into countless, smaller streams and rivers. In the evening sun's reflection, there was a glistening of water as far south and east as my eyes could focus. Not being much of a traveler, I did feel privileged at that moment to be seeing what was soon to be the entire bird world's rest and recovery rookery. [ed.

note: Seasonal "R and R" to some of you out there.] Already the sky was repeatedly blackened with raucous, migrating flocks of birds of all descriptions and sizes. Even as far away and as early in the process as I was, looking down from my vantage point, I could hear the din of billions of birds, arguing, greeting, counting, shouting and singing. It had become the most remarkable, worldly chorus ever assembled in one place. And sadly, I realized that probably this was the last year that something of this size would take place for many years to come, if ever again.

Just at the point I was about to become immersed in that haunting and overwhelming prospect, I heard a call come from overhead; and I looked up.

"Are you the fellow that we're supposed to meet up with today?" a very large, all white bird yelled down at me.

"Maybe," I replied. "Who said you were to do so?" I countered.

"It was a pair of doomsday-prophesying loons. I believe they said their names were Lance and Lolly," came the welcome answer.

"Then, yes, I am that individual. And who is it I am addressing?"

"Well, most folks call me 'Stan', and given the circumstances we appear to be facing in the near future, I guess you can do the same."

"Certainly, Stan," I complied. "Are there others like you who are also planning to attend the meeting that I presume Lance and Lolly also told you about?"

"Yes, there are ninety-seven more besides me coming; seven pairs of seven different varieties of us in all."

"Good," I answered, relieved that Lolly and Lance's message was being broadcast accurately. Likewise, as I noted from Stan's answer, the follow-up, so far, was as it should be. "What you might do now," I then added, "is simply follow me a short way further along this hilltop. I don't intend to descend down off this ridgeline into the greenbelt below, if it's not necessary. Thick, jungle brush makes me nervous; I can get lost quite easily in confined areas."

"Hey, in that respect, you and I have something in common," the very large stork, who was now simply gliding along about ten feet above me, concurred. "I'm much better finding my way up here. Put me down there in all that, and I'd be lost in seconds as well. Besides, I don't walk too gracefully. It's my beak; it seems to always get in the way as I try to maneuver through thickets. It snags up. Actually, it's simply too long, but what can you do?"

"I know," I answered, relieved that he was not a stuffed-shirt kind of bird. I was already beginning to like him. "I feel the same about some of my so-called attributes: my general appearance for one. Look at my ears! They just lay there. Most folks either don't have any or they stand up perfectly erect all the time. Mine just drape down over the side of my head. And I've got the memory of a rock. I can't even remember when yesterday was."

Obviously becoming more comfortable with what he was hearing, Stan then asked my name, and from then on, for the next hour, we chatted as I scampered along to the final place for the upcoming meeting. It made the final trek less tiresome and gave me a much needed boost in my confidence for what was ahead.

And in less than an hour after Stan and I arrived at the spot where I had instructed Lance and Lolly to tell everyone we should rendezvous, the area was overflowing with the ninety-seven other birds. It was obvious by all the chatter, the two of them had briefly described the urgency of each pair needing to come here.

When it was clear to me that all the birds had arrived and were settled down somewhat, I cleared my throat and started my monologue. But their animated conversations didn't seem to stop, some of which involved their yearly, reunion gossip. Finally, I yelled, "Will you stop talking and listen to me!!? I need everyone's attention right now!!!"

It was Lance who then whispered up inside my ear flap that it might help if I climbed up on top of a small knoll at the northern edge of the assembly area. Working my way through the maze of birds, who now seemed to have been stunned into silence, I scampered up a small rise and was able to look down on all of them.

"Forgive my shouting, but we must hurry. There is an urgency associated with what you are about to do that cannot be overstated." And it was at that moment that the ground, for the first time that I could ever remember, began to rumble and shake a little. That only rattled me more. It seemed to me later like some all-seeing **Force** was adding more drama to what I was about to say.

Someone in the audience, seeing my surprise and rising fear, shouted, "That's nothing, Mack. You should feel what I and my kin have experienced further north of here. There is such shaking that none of our eggs hatched this year. They were all broken. And we understand that is happening everywhere. That's what all our talk was about, when you halted us. We were sharing with one another our experiences and the loss of an entire generation of young'uns. Some of us have even witnessed the ground splitting open. All that coupled with the gathering blackness and raging noise that sits off shorelines everywhere, has all of us spooked. What's happening?" [ed. note: This is the first primary documentation ever found of the beginning separation of the super continent into its major subcontinents.]

This development was the introduction I needed for what I was about to tell them. It wasn't until afterwards that the impact of the ground shaking and dividing, along with the impending storm fronts rose fully into my consciousness. At that point an almost paralyzing fear gripped me. But until then, I reviewed with them what Lance and Lolly had obviously told them, then I proceeded to outline what I needed them to do immediately.

Basically, I requested that they develop a plan on how to circulate amongst all the birds that were arriving in the expanse below us and give them definite instructions on what they needed to do. Then I asked some of them to fly to wherever there are any bird species that do not routinely migrate to this area and inform them as well. And finally I instructed them that they would need to do the same for any and all animals in this region and between here and wherever they are from. They were to tell every living species of bird and animal that up to seven pair of them needed to assemble at Noah's place six months from today.

In addition, I outlined that one pair each of twenty specific animal and bird species needed to be notified they were to be at Noah's in one month's time, and that they must be prepared to stay there through the boat's launching and sailing. This last, designated group was to be chosen from the five distinct areas of our landmass [ed. note: As you know better than I, these are the "areas", which are now distinctly separated and are called Europe, North and South America, Asia, Australia and Africa.] These twenty representatives were each to be assigned to a specific committee, of which there would be four. In conclusion, I then told them that these same representatives would be given instructions about their particular duties after their arrival at Noah's.

Following my lengthy speech, there was another hour of questions and discussion. But through it all, it was clear that Lance and Lolly had chosen well. There was no haggling or argument about what was happening. Everyone, by then, particularly these birds who had witnessed the gathering storm fronts, knew something terrible was about to happen to us all. Encouraged by their determination and willingness to spend the next six months being Messengers to the world, I concluded the meeting, assuring each of them, wherever possible each pair of them would be accompanying Noah on his and his family's boat ride into whatever future might lay ahead for any of us.

The meeting ended solemnly. No doubt, a prayer of some kind was in order, but I knew none. It wasn't something Holly and I practiced in our daily lives. We didn't know how to. But given the grave circumstances ahead, it was clear at that moment that there were no non-believers in that crowd before me nor any in any assembly I would be in ever after that.

EIGHT: THE COMMITTEES

My trip back to Holly went fast. And I mean fast. I found some vines that I could weave into a kind of rope, which I tied around my waist. I know I was supposed to get a belt before I left home for that purpose, but as I've already said, I often forget things. Anyhow, I tied it in place; then stuck the shepherd's staff through it, positioning it across my back with the crook hanging over my left shoulder as I ran along. True, the tip of the crook occasionally touched the ground and startled me, but overall I was able to make great time, and it only took me a day and a half to reach home.

My reunion with Holly was joyful. With all that had happened both between her and Noah, the individuals who I kept sending back to meet with her during my journey and my stories of what I saw, heard and felt, we were busy talking for hours. Finally, by sunrise on the thirteenth day since Noah first informed me about what was going to occur, Holly and I climbed out of our burrow, and she pointed down toward Noah's farm to see what had been happening there.

To my absolute amazement I could actually see something very large laid out on his biggest pasture area. The building process had actually begun. They were no longer just cutting and shaping logs. Excited by it all, I decided to head down there immediately. She had to go anyway, because it was now her daily routine to spend at least six to eight hours helping Nora and her family prepare and wrap food supplies for the boat trip. And over the days I had been gone, Holly had even coaxed about a dozen of our closest relatives to help out as well. So, as the sun rose over our range of hills, the collection of us, some running, some walking, and a few, like me, just ambling along, descended down to Nora and Noah's for a day of work and more revelations.

For me, the first revelation was how much Noah's crew had accomplished in the three or four weeks since he had initially started building the boat. The keel was now laid out, all six hundred feet of it. And on top of that were being attached the twelve-inch square cants for the bottom deck section. Most amazing of all was that Elaine and Elliot had been able to enlist the services of ten of their herd members to come and help as well. As trees were felled, trimmed of branches and sectioned, one of their cousins, nephews, brothers or sisters would lift them with their trunk and bring them out into the large clearing to be shaped into cants and then gouged and bored to fashion the mortise and tenons. It was a well-oiled machine to watch. Other elephants were taking the finished cants over to the keel section and laying them alongside the others that had been fixed into place on the keel stringers.

There were no sides, bow or stern sections being erected yet, Noah explained to me. Everyone agreed the lower deck section had to be locked down first. Then the outline of the superstructure would begin being built. [ed. note: Think of the early pioneers framing barns with huge timbers.] The sounds of chopping, hammering, scraping and chiseling were just about all one heard. Only occasionally would you notice some instruction being given or a private conversation, but it was always brief. And that went on day and night.

After Noah showed me this building process, he then pulled me over to the side of the construction area and pointed to the fence line bordering the road, which led to the various towns in the neighborhood. It was crammed with people. It even looked as if the wooden fencing was beginning to lean backward towards us. Noah and his family had embedded wooden posts every six feet, with three staggered cross-boards lashed down between each of them. By then, they were beginning to heave under the ever-growing public, pushing and shoving to get a better view of what was happening.

"Where are Lois and Lewis, Elaine and Elliott?" I inquired, somewhat puzzled and alarmed.

"Oh, they are in the area," Noah calmly reassured me. "Every now and then, one of them or a couple of the other less cordial Guardians will make a sweep of the area. Whenever Roy the Rhino, Benton the Buffalo, or Homer the Hippo, makes their hourly tour, the crowd edges backward, away from the fence. Otherwise, they and all the other Guardians are scattered throughout the property that surrounds us. You'll see the chimps running back and forth delivering messages to the others. It is a vigil they all take quite seriously. And, for now, the crowd seems to respect them. But what worries me is that daily I see more new faces arriving. The number of onlookers continues to grow in size and volume. Who knows what will happen by the time we are ready for launch?"

"Have you felt any of the ground-shaking?" I then asked.

"Yes, a little," he replied, somewhat surprised at my asking. "We've wondered what it was all about. Do you have any clue what may be causing it? Did anyone amongst the many creatures you met and talked to know or see anything out of the ordinary where they came from?"

"Hasn't anyone told you?" I exclaimed.

"About   what?"

"About the storms gathering, stretching along the entire shoreline, surrounding the land we stand on, and the violent shaking and splitting open of the ground throughout the world?"

"No," came his suddenly grave reply. "Tell me what you've heard."

And for the next hour, sitting not too far from the building site, I gave Noah a complete report of everything that happened to me, and what I was told, since I last saw him. It left him visibly shaken.

Seeing his reaction shook me. Don't ever

get the impression I'm a brave soldier. I'm not. Fear and hunger are my two closest companions, aside from Holly. I do try to appear vigilant and brave; it's an act. And I'm nervous, and I worry, which doesn't help matters. I would be the last one pictured on a recruitment poster, asking for brave volunteers for dangerous duty somewhere in the world. I startle and spook easily. I need reassurance often from Holly. In truth, I'm the last choice that Noah should have made for what I am attempting to do for him. How and why he chose me, the very least of creatures, is a mystery, and that, too, worries me. My constant worry is 'when will I fail him', and likely miserably so. I know it is coming; it always does. How could I comfort and reassure Noah, seeing him like this?

We ultimately agreed that only Nora and Holly should be made aware of these developments for the time being. The sense of desperation and futility that could result from his family and the local animals being told these awesome portents could paralyze the preparations now underway. Both of us hated the secrecy and hoped that before long this news could be circulated amongst everyone; they deserved to know. For now, preparing for what lay ahead trumped full disclosure, but this is always a slippery surface to make a stand on. Leadership anywhere and everywhere hides behind such decisions. Neither of us left that debriefing comfortable nor secure in our knowledge or with that decision. Maybe being truly humbled and thoroughly frightened are partial penalties and serve to remind one that secrets in times of great stress and shared commitment to a cause are best kept to a minimum and are to be divulged to all as soon as possible.

Shaking his head as he walked away, Noah called out to me to double check how the Guardians were managing, and to see if they needed reinforcements or supplies. It was a few days later that I suggested that he and I spend more time with the Guardians, keeping them updated on developments and the progress of meeting certain timelines and schedules. Also, at this meeting, I informed him of some details about the types and composition of the Committees that he and one or more of his family might have to help chair.

And to finish out that first day back from the Delta, I searched for Lois and Lewis to get their impressions on how their task of protecting the compound was going. Finding them in the back portion of Noah's property wasn't an easy task. If they didn't want to be seen, you didn't find them. And they were taking a nap, waiting their turn at patrolling the property's perimeter. Up until that meeting with them, I had no idea how big Nora and Noah's property was.

It was one parcel, 640 acres or one square mile with 5280 feet to a side, and it was perfectly square. Their property sat in the middle of a large valley, with the stream I bathed in running through it. It was an immense area for Lois and Lewis to supervise patrolling. So much so, that without asking me or Noah, they enlisted twelve more of their relatives and asked each of the other members on the Guardian team to do the same. That brought the total number of those protecting Noah and his family to 98! (Coincidentally, I had just recently recruited the same number of Messengers.) And as I inspected the perimeter with the two, you could already see a pathway being worn behind the fence line.

But, luckily, it was overall, a large enough area that each Guardian couple and the thousands of birds and animals that were to eventually arrive could find a measure of privacy in the woods that were contained in Nora and Noah's then-designated compound. And believe me; 'time out' space was needed. Already, there were arguments having to be settled within the Guardians. I couldn't imagine what the magnitude of the problems would be when every living creature of any size was living for weeks or months aboard an enclosed, cramped boat.

And as it turned out, Lewis informed me he already had a problem that needed to be resolved. Benton, the Cape buffalo, wanted to be in charge; and he was scheming and plotting to overthrow Lewis and Lois' supervisory roles and my tenuous excuse for authority. A meeting had to be called right away, with Noah and all his family in attendance. We arranged to have it the next night, just before shift change. It would take a day to notify everyone to attend. And it would be mandatory.

And it was during that same meeting that I outlined for everyone what Committees were going to be organized and who was to be on them. I figured it was as good a time as any to get that news out, and let the fur, feathers and hair fly.

So by 6 p.m., two weeks after Noah first drafted me into this desperate operation, all 98 Guardians, 14 meerkats and Noah's 31 family members, for a grand total of 144 hard-toiling and highly stressed workers, gathered for our First Update Meeting, as Noah would describe them. And one of our 144 members had a growing urge to make trouble. (Intrigue seems to be found wherever two or more are gathered together, no matter their genus or species.) Knowing that and attempting to maintain a brave front, I nodded to Noah that it was clear that everyone had arrived, and he rose to speak.

"Nora, family, friends, neighbors and newly arrived Guardians," he began. "Certain news has come to my attention during the last twenty-four hours that warranted this meeting. However, even if there were no matters needing to be addressed immediately, it seems appropriate to have a meeting such as this periodically, to give each of you the opportunity to offer suggestions and to ask questions. We have entered into completely uncharted territory. None of us knows what is going to happen in the days, weeks and months that are to come. And certainly issues and concerns during that time span will arise that we should address promptly.

"So to start with, let me give any of you an opportunity to rise and express an opinion or raise an issue of concern. Just raise your hand, stand or speak out, whatever is necessary, to get my attention. Anyone?"

There followed a period of some

restlessness, with most of us turning our heads to see if someone was standing or raising their hand. There was no one. At least not until there was a shuffling and movement from the back of the audience. Mind you, we were all sitting or standing on the unfinished lower deck or on the keel stringers of that immense, maybe-eventually-going-to-be-a boat. We were looking west toward Noah and his son's cottages and barns, as the sun was squeezing down between the high hillsides in front of us; and luckily, there was still about one hour of daylight left when Noah called the meeting to order. And in unison, everyone turned in that fading light to see who was about to speak.

From the rear and to the left side of the audience a booming voice yelled, "I have a suggestion and a request."

Craning his neck to see clearly who called out, Noah nodded, unsurprised at who had just spoken and replied, "Yes, Benton, what is on your mind?"

"I feel that your choices of organizer and supervisors of the Guardians are lacking in authority, at least in the first instance, and in all likelihood are suffering from favoritism in the second. Merrill is not suited for the job. He is neither large enough nor strong enough. And Lewis and Lois are being shown deferential treatment. I'd like to offer my services in both these capacities, which would make any future problem or matter easier for you to address if they should arise."

"Thank you, Benton, for raising this issue," Noah politely began. "It highlights something that really does need to be clarified tonight. And that is, 'how did I determine who was to help direct this undertaking?' It was based solely on trust. It had nothing to do with size or physical strength. The mammoth job we have before us will require that each of us give and endure conditions and circumstances far beyond anything we ever thought imaginable. I cannot even begin to picture in my mind what lays ahead for all of us. But if at any time, any of us here have an issue with the leadership or the direction this project is taking, we will call a meeting such as this and vote on it. Whenever possible, we will strive to be democratic and let the majority determine what should be done, as cumbersome and sometimes dangerous and confusing as that process can become. It would be much easier for me to just issue edicts and let the matter stand, with no discussion or voting, such as I had to do when I selected Merrill and Holly to help me and my family. There simply was no other option for me then.

"So now, let's vote on whether Merrill should keep his position and whether it was a good choice for him to have Lois and Lewis be the supervisors of the Guardians, with Elliot and Elaine as their backup supervisors. All in favor of the matter standing as is, please raise your hands, paws, hooves, wings, trunks or tails."

And to my utter amazement, there were 123 votes in support of the status quo. Noah, Holly, the two lions and elephants and I abstained, while all fourteen of the Cape buffalo voted "no".

"From what I count, Benton, your concern is

not shared by most everyone else here," Noah observed. "But I certainly will make it a point to monitor closely the effectiveness of their work. Are there any other issues tonight we need to address?"

I could tell by looking over at Benton that this voting had not satisfied his desire to take charge of things. But it appeared he chose not to press the matter.

I felt a distinct threat building. It was one of those premonition things that all folks have, even us that walk or run with our bellies much closer to the ground.

Just then Holly looked over at me and nodded, in an overt expression of agreement with my unspoken concern. We had to be watchful. A world-covering Flood was to be the least of our worries in the immediate future; we were sure of that.

However, there were no other issues or concerns raised from the audience. That left the rest of the meeting open to discussions about the progress of the boat building, with an emphasis on cutting and shaping logs faster, if that was at all possible; discussions over getting supplies assembled and better organized for the actual trip, and having Noah's family begin to fashion thick ropes for raising the framing and decking to the upper levels..

Just before the meeting ended, Noah finally turned to me and asked me to brief everyone on the Committees and the composition of each. Somewhat reluctantly, after hearing Benton's objection to my role in helping Noah, and in an attempt to be as concise as possible, I then gave a brief outline of each one, including their respective members and their functions. I did not know individual names at that time, but I supply them now for this record. [ed. note: This is the first recorded, practical use of the word "committee"[1] and the subsequent follow-through with the formation of one. The success or failure of what followed Merrill's use of them most likely played a significant role in shaping the world that arose after the *Second Beginning*...]   They are as listed below:

    1. Prearrival Planning:
        A. Membership
            (and region represented):
            • Local: Noah, Nora, Holly and myself.
            • Australia: Kelly, a male kangaroo. [ed. note: Please take special notice that the names of subcontinents preceded their drifting apart from the super continent, Pangaea. Modern-day folks always seem to think they are the first to name

---

[1] "Committee:-as applied to a body" (in contrast to an individual): "A body of two or more persons" (and various animals and birds) "appointed or elected by a society, corporation, public meeting, etc." (or a meerkat...), "for some special business or function.." The Oxford English Dictionary, Oxford University Press. Oxford. 1971.

everything. Just goes to show you...]
- Europe: Helen, a female hoopoe (bird).
- Asia: Perry, a male giant Chinese panda.
- Africa: Karen, a female Botswana kudu (animal).
- North/South America: Terry, a male keel-billed Bolivian toucan.

B. Functions:

- Design and prepare distinct campsite areas for animals and birds from each region. This will allow staged mingling and acceptance of one another from all regions, thereby avoiding unnecessary territorial disputes, particularly when everyone is crammed together into Noah's bobbing, wooden, oversized box.
- Establish methods for collecting, processing and storage of food supplies for each person, animal and bird for the boat trip and for one year following its final docking.
- Try to figure out how in the world we are to gather seeds and plants from all the different species over the entire world...Whose's idea was that!!!? Come on, give it a break!!....Weren't trying to gather all the birds and animals enough?!!!
- Organize who will help with

completing construction of the boat and what they will be doing..

2. Arrival/Settling in Prior to Sailing:

A. Membership:
- Local: Noah, Ham and myself.
- Australia: Millie, a female magpie.
- Europe: Todd, a male Scottish Terrier.
- Asia: Patience, a female Indian Peacock.
- North/South America: Ian, a male green Amazonian iguana.
- Africa: Fern, a female lesser Kenyan flamingo.

B. Functions:
- Finalize the actual number of each animal and bird who is sailing.
- Complete plans and furnishings for the interior of the boat, e.g. roosts for birds to be stretched and staggered across the width of the boat in each compartment and simulated tree limbs for animals with special needs erected in each compartment.
- Decide who and what goes where on the various decks.
- Establish rules for proper manners, schedules for meals, ideas for recreational activities, guidelines for daily private matters, and corrective actions for unruly or

disruptive behavior.
3. The Voyage:
   A. Membership:
   - Local: Noah, Nora, Shem and myself.
   - Australia: Glenda, a female sugar glider (animal).
   - Europe: Carl, a male cuckoo.
   - Asia: Olive, a female Indonesian orangutan.
   - North/South America: Paula, a female macaw parrot.
   - Africa: Graham, a male low land Congolese gorilla. [ed. note: Are you getting the picture by now? See, there is little new under the Sun…even the country names were in common use during those much earlier times.]
   B. Functions:
   - Arbitrate and settle disputes regarding territorial and food issues.
   - Provide shipboard entertainment to combat dangerous boredom.
   - Set watches and duty rosters.
   - Hopefully provide for some navigation input, rather than just bob along. See if there is any way to steer the boat once it is afloat…
   - Determine the process for exiting the boat, as opposed to it being a general stampede when we finally have the opportunity to permanently

leave Noah's ark.

4. Resettlement;
    A. Membership:
        - Local: Noah, Japheth, Holly and myself.
        - Australia: Kyle, a male kookaburra.
        - Europe: Bertha, a female bison.
        - Asia: Stan, a male stork.
        - North/South America: Lily, a female Peruvian llama.
        - Africa: Barclay, a male red and yellow barket (bird).
    B. Functions:
        - Determine who goes where, when and what they take with them.
        - Ensure a safe exit off boat, avoiding trampling.
        - Provide predetermined food distribution to everyone for their upcoming years' survival.
        - Emphasize that everyone needs to be present for Noah's final address, before we are ultimately dispersed throughout the world.

Then, after nearly another hours' discussing of these Committee matters, Noah concluded our first meeting with these words.

"Folks, none of us here tonight have any idea how all this is going to turn out. And probably we will not have any idea from this moment on, to the end of our pending voyage. We had only the most rudimentary directions given us in what to build and what to load onto it. We have no timelines or other guidelines. This is an uncharted and unprecedented venture. I am expecting major conflict and hysteria as the climate changes and the rain begins. We must prepare for that, as well as for the voyage itself. There will be a massive influx of life coming to this place from all corners of the world in about six months. To prepare for that, members of Merrill's various Committees should be arriving in the next month. My plan is to have each of us scattered throughout our property, in hopes of letting us become acquainted slowly and cordially. Unrest and conflict amongst us will be disastrous and will require the sternest measures to avoid. Be patient. Be strong. And be ever prayerful, whoever or whatever you are."

Four weeks later, the Committee members began to arrive.

NINE: THE PASSENGERS

Unfortunately, it wasn't long after the arrival of all the Committee members (and the time it took me to get them settled into the various areas around Noah and Nora's property, and then to have them meet the members of their respective committees and have our first preliminary meetings) that I personally experienced the first, but certainly not the last, great shock and the feeling of being threatened.

About eight weeks after Noah first alerted me about what was going to happen, as dictated to him by the **Floodmaster**, I was strolling along Nora's and his fence line at the rear of their property. On that morning, Benton and his band had been assigned to protect that area, but oddly, there was no one around. At least there was no one that I could see, which was not unusual, as I've mentioned before. I just figured they were camouflaged and observing the surroundings from the wooded areas. I was very wrong.

Suddenly, from a fifty foot swath of the guarded perimeter, there came a charge of at least thirty to forty townsfolk. Sooner than I could react in any sensible manner, they had knocked down fence slats with mallets and long, thick poles. They meant business and nothing was going to get in their way. Catching sight of me, one of them shouted out, "There's one of the ring-leaders, let's finish him off first! That will send a clear message to these thieving mongrels!! We've all had enough of this secret society business! Get him!! We'll string him up on a tree once we get to the clearing where that monstrosity is being built. Enough is enough!!"

And before I could react, I was grabbed by two or three of the burliest folks I'd ever seen. I knew then that my time on this world was over. I hated that I wouldn't get a chance to at least tell Holly "good-bye". But that was about the only thought I had. I was scared witless. And I felt that at any minute my neck was going to be twisted like a helpless chicken, or that I would be banged in the head with a club as if I was some petrified ground squirrel.

In my panic, I was just about to pass out, when all of a sudden there arose from around me a roar that seemed to fill that entire valley. It rolled up one side of the surrounding hillsides and down the other. It charged the air so much, every hair on my body stood straight up. I looked like a porcupine, dangling down from some goon's greasy hands. Immediately, this odd assortment of humanity froze in place, as approaching them, crouched and steadily slinking forward were Lewis, Lois and the other twelve of their band of lions. To them this was no staged drama. This intruding mob was beginning to look like a nice brunch, and I wasn't sure a massacre wasn't about to happen.

Suddenly, the clown that shouted for everyone to surround and take me hostage called out, "Hold on! We meant no harm. This was just a game we play with each other. Honest. We weren't going to hurt your furry friend here; believe me!"

In retaliation, before the fellow holding me could let go, I spun around, doubled up and bit his hand as hard as I could. He screamed and flung me over the heads of the other intruders.

Landing on the ground near Lewis, Lois then turned to me and asked, "Are you ok? Do you want us to dine on a couple of these varmints anyway? We would, you know."

"No, no," I protested. "Noah and Nora would be very upset if you did that. But we do need to ensure that they are convinced not to try this again. Instead, you should scare them pantless."

So with more roaring, jumping up and down, pawing the air and, most frightening of all, opening their immense jaws and flashing the countless number of their chisel-sharp teeth, the invaders fell over themselves trying to escape before being eaten alive. We didn't see any of them again...until months later.

But that left unanswered why this area had been left unguarded, with no patrols even remotely in the vicinity. Upon questioning me, Lewis deduced that I regularly took this morning stroll; it was a predictable pattern for me. Then he thought of the first meeting we had with everyone, in which

Noah and Benton, the Cape buffalo, had their exchange of views. A possible link to what happened that day was forming in his mind.

However, it was decided to let the matter settle somewhat before pursuing it with Noah. No sense jumping to conclusions. We were all going to have to be living together in extremely close quarters before too long, and it made no sense to alienate each other unnecessarily.

That decided, Lois hurried back to the boat area and let Noah know that the fencing needed to be repaired. The other lions remained there to ensure there weren't other people waiting to breach the fence's perimeter. And I decided to continue my walk. I needed to. I was a nervous wreck, and the walk would help calm me down before I got back to Holly.

But that was another mistake. Once I had walked a quarter mile from that area, I was confronted by Benton, standing in the middle of the path. And it was obvious he knew about the just-stymied invasion attempt. Along with him were the thirteen others of his kind. I knew the jig was up this time for sure.

"Think you're so smart, don't you?!" he yelled.

Me? So smart? That shows how dumb he was. That feeling was as alien to me as thinking I could one day be an Olympic swimmer. Smart, I ain't. Scared, I was.

I simply replied, quivering as I did, "No, I don't."

"Well, it's over for you, as of right now," he

bellowed, assuming a stance that indicated a lethal charge was about to take place. "This entire venture of your preparations and boat building is going to end. Nothing is going to happen, anyway. It's all a farce, meant to scare us. It's simply a plot to capture assorted animals and various birds. Well, it's not happening, and you're going to be the first one to know it!!"

But again, there erupted a series of fearsome roars that stunned me. Apparently, Lewis had been following me, secreted in the wooded area along the path. But as his needed backup this time, Elliot, Elaine and their twelve other family members had also been monitoring the buffalo herd all morning. With trunks upright, they charged full-steam, straight into them.

Believe me, nothing alters someone's smoldering resentments or festering plots like experiencing a herd of charging elephants, led by a 500 pound, open-mouthed lion.

More fencing was bowled-over that morning, as the buffalo herd was last seen scampering over the eastern hillsides. And that was the end of the Benton era. Later on, I was able to arrange with Lance and Lolly, my two recruiting loons, to locate another pair of Cape buffalo for Noah. But they were to look in an altogether different region for them this time.

And it was while making this request of them, which came two weeks after the fracas with Benton and his bunch of bums, that the three of us decided that we needed to meet with Noah and Nora as well. During that meeting with all five of us, it was determined that the loons should return here to update Noah and myself at least once each month for the next four months. It would keep us posted on any untoward events or developments prior to the final migration to our location. We needed to be apprised of any problems and the progress that was being made. There were too many reasons, most totally unknowable, for this earthly migration to fail.

And, without question, the next meeting with the loons was a watershed event. It came three months into the six month period that notification and collection of the world's other animal and bird inhabitants was taking place. And it also marked a major milestone in the construction of Noah's boat. It was decided to have everyone presently staying and working at Nora and Noah's attend this Second Update Meeting. At that time, everyone could participate in revising any goals or suggest new ones that the Prearrival Planning Committee should consider.

Noah spoke first, as was expected. And he noted that with the addition of many townsfolk to help with tree cutting and shaping the fallen timber into the proper lengths, sizes and shapes, the construction was moving faster than expected. The boat's superstructure was now all in place, with more than half the decking already laid and secured. It was expected that the deck laying process would be even faster, given that they were no longer having to make so many cants and were now shifting to making more boards. Furthermore, it had been decided that a one hundred foot ramp would be constructed and secured on the top deck, adjacent to the ramp entrance, near which it would be lowered and raised. It would rest on the top deck during the voyage, as a result of the boat conveniently being exactly one hundred feet wide. The ramp's surface planking would have cross-pieces secured every twelve inches along its length to allow for safer footing. This was because there would be a 45 degree angle that everyone would have to climb and, if we lived long enough, to descend. In that regard, the interior ramps, connecting each of the four decks, would then be constructed and secured in place along the boat's midsection. Once the top deck's planking was in place, that deck would be the first to be coated with pitch and resin to seal the top of the boat. Next, the lower deck or Deck #4, followed by the stern, bow, starboard and port sides would be waterproofed. To complete the construction phase, the interior modifications and additions would then be added. And following that, only then would supplies start being loaded onto Deck #4 at the bow end of the boat.

Noah then asked Karen, the African kudu, to come forward to speak for the Committee. Immediately upon his turning to face the audience, she began by describing the areas throughout Nora and Noah's back property that had been cordoned off for the newcomers who would be arriving from the five major regions. Each area would allow enough room for the newly arrived inhabitants to have some space for themselves, and then to become acquainted with their fellow, regional nationals at a somewhat modest pace. Leisure time for becoming familiar with everyone else from the other regions would probably be a luxury. The only hope she expressed was that the new arrivals would at least become comfortably acquainted with their fellow bunk mates.

Recently, she noted agreements had been reached on the deck assignments of the regional passengers and of Noah's family within the boat. Supplies would be stored in one-half of Deck #4. And as previously mentioned by Noah, they would be in the bow portion. Housed in the other half of that deck would be the animals and birds from both Asia and Europe. But it was noted that many birds, from all regions, would probably spend a lot of their time on Deck #1, the top one, for obvious reasons.

Deck #3 would be divided equally for passengers from Africa in the bow section, from Australia in the mid section and those from North/South America in the stern section. And the bow section of Deck #2 would house Nora and Noah and their families, and all the large animals from everywhere would be in its stern section. [ed. note: See the accompanying Appendix: "CUT-AWAY SKETCH OF THE FIRST ARK"] It was decided that anyone weighing more than 200 pounds was considered to be a "large animal" and should be allowed to bunk in the stern portion of Deck #2. Lighter animals could scamper up all the deck ramps quicker and safer, in the case of personal emergencies or late night Restroom Facility "calls", as we soon termed them. Under no circumstance was anyone to relieve themselves anywhere but in the Restroom Facilities, except, of course, for the majority of the birds on board. They were still allowed to fly.

There then followed a lengthy discussion between Karen, the members of her committee, the two loons and Nora about collecting food supplies and getting them delivered to our location. It was decided that Lance and Lolly would spread the word for any bird who was big enough to help load onto the boat any size sack they could manage, filled with grain, seeds, or small plants. Anyone bringing food supplies from the five regions were to transport them to the two barns that Noah and his sons had built years ago. Their own, personal animals, which had been stabled inside each of them were now tethered outside, and the two barns had been thoroughly scrubbed and prepared to safely accept and store foodstuffs. Lolly mentioned that the various South American and African monkeys that had already arrived at the Delta Assembly area were peeling and preparing a wide variety of fruits and vegetables to dry for the boat trip. Likewise, bushels of corn kernels were being brought by the South American contingent, and every other animal of any size was to be transporting grasses, seeds and plants from their home locations.

But NO ONE had any idea how to collect and save the seedlings, bulbs and seeds from "ALL THE PLANTS IN THE WORLD"!!! That came as no surprise to me. It was not like there was a Pangaea Catalog you could use to order everything for express mail delivery to Noah's. Lance noted that everyone was instructed to bring what that could as they journeyed to the Delta. But there was no way to determine if all the species "out there" were found or saved. There wasn't time. There weren't the personnel. And, frankly, there just wasn't the motivation.

First off, you're scared spitless from being told that the end of all known life is about to occur, then you see storm fronts gather that stretch beyond anything you've ever imagined and the earth is cracking open and shaking almost constantly. Then you're told to gather your partner, some supplies and fly, crawl, climb, run or walk halfway around the world to a place called "Okavango". And "Oh, by the way, would you collect all the plants and seeds in your neighborhood and bring them along with you, as well!!"

Noah could only add that we had to do the best we could and guessed we'd have to leave it at that.

Karen's summary concluded with an invitation for any and all animals that could be helpful in the construction process, e.g. smearing pitch along the lower and upper decks and up and down the boat's four sides, to volunteer helping Noah and his family. But even then it was noted that many were already showing up daily for such duty without being asked.

Finally, Lance and Lolly reported that the different species were arriving daily from all corners of Pangaea. The Messengers were doing a splendid job of spreading the word in all directions. And they expected that everyone possible would have been notified by now. What remained was for those told at the furthest distance to make their way to the Delta over these final three months. And they concluded with grave remarks about the continued darkening, boiling and deafening storm fronts that encircled the world. No one could see the tops of the cloud formations any longer. They appeared to be rising endlessly. And the earthquakes were more violent and now seemed to be continuous in some places. Only this particular region appeared to be spared this naturally occurring violence.

After everyone who needed to speak had done so, and after each item was then thoroughly discussed, the meeting was adjourned. It took over four hours for everyone to have their say and input. And while it was sobering to most, it was absolutely terrifying to me. Hearing what Lance and Lolly were being told made my knees knock. Something horrific was about to occur. Everyone felt it. And it goaded us into working even more diligently in the weeks and months left.

Next, I'm left to describe for you what happened during the final week of that six month deadline as the remaining animals and birds arrived. The first to arrive were the birds. They were led by Lance and Lolly and were herded, if you will, by the Messengers on the outside perimeter of a mammoth, sky-darkening riot of these birds. There were all sizes, shapes, colors and sounds represented. It was like a thousand rainbows were singing, chirping and calling, as they blotted-out the blue sky. It was a wonder of wonders to me. And just to highlight their accomplishment, Lolly and

Lance piloted this soaring throng in circles above Nora and Noah's estate seven times. It stopped all work and brought all workers and citizens along the fence line to a complete halt. Eyes were pointed skyward for the next thirty minutes. I've never seen anything like it before or since, in terms of sheer beauty.

Then, as if directed by the most commanding conductor, the chorus dived earthward in five separate groups, again led by the Messengers to their respective regional sites within the wooded area behind the boat. And in that instant, the rush of feathers, wings and song stopped and it was quiet, except for the panting of the many witnesses to this marvel. Every species of bird on Pangaea had now arrived for the eventual boarding on Noah's boat, which was to come in the not too distant future.

But it wasn't like many of them hadn't already been there. The shuttle of food and different species of plants and seed had been ongoing for the last three months. But this was the final and most spectacular, full-dress parade of them all together. It took Holly's and my breath away to watch it unfold.

Two days later, appearing over the eastern, grassy hillsides behind Nora and Noah's place, a low rumble was heard. It grew in volume, as something of great size approached. Next, just before anything appeared at the top ridgeline, the ground beneath all of us began to quiver and shake. Of course, my first impression was that it was another of those earthquakes that I felt on my trip to the Delta. But this was much, much stronger. And it frightened me. Holly and I, standing outside our burrow, looked at each other with concern and growing panic.

Then, as if on cue, the entire one mile ridgeline immediately behind Noah's property was filled with the heads and bodies of countless animals of all sizes and description. Some were riding on the backs of others. The various species were not clumped together, but had scattered amongst the onrushing herd. Gangly giraffe's heads and necks could be seen scattered haphazardly throughout the mass of animals. And as they began to descend down the hillside, a cloud of dust rose as the numbers of animals flowed onward towards us. Leading it all were Lewis and Lois, who apparently had left a few days ago to escort everyone here.

This overpowering entry created an almost celebratory mood, which given the soon-to-be tragic reason for their coming here, should have been almost funerary. In a way, this surging panorama seemed to say that life would prevail, even given the circumstances that were causing such a massive extinction to occur. None of these representatives had a sense of self-pride of being chosen to come here. Their selection was a matter of sheer luck. Their energetic appearance that day was driven by their knowing that their particular species did have a slim chance, but at least a chance, of continuing to live in another time and place.

The heaving mass of animals slowed down to a walk by the time they reached Noah's property. Lewis and Lois had seen to it that Ham had removed about 100 feet of fencing to allow passage into the property and their immediate disbursement to the five regional, relocation centers. Within two hours of first sighting the thundering hordes, everyone was settled. All the birds and animals from Asia, Europe, North/South America, Africa and Australia were now camped in separate areas, waiting the time they would be told to climb the ramp into Noah's ark.

EMBARKATION

TEN: LAST MINUTE DETAILS

Holly and I were so excited about the arrival of everyone; we sat up all that same night reviewing what had happened over the last few days. By dawn the next morning I still hadn't had any urge to sleep, so I decided to start my morning rounds of the building site, fence line and the regional, relocation and bivouac areas. Thinking it would probably take me a few hours to do this, seeing how it would be the first day all the animals and birds had finally resettled here at Noah and Nora's, I slipped out of our burrow earlier than usual and tried not to awaken Holly.

No sooner had I walked into the boat building area when Noah's booming voice hailed me. "Merrill! Just who I needed to see the first thing today! Can I borrow a few minutes of your time, so early this morning?"

"Sure thing, chief," I happily replied. "What's on your mind?"

"We've got to hurry things along," he

began. "I had another Visitation from the Floodmaster, as you describe the Creator and Lord of All."

"What happened?" I asked, now beginning to lose some of my earlier jolliness. *In those days being happy was a very temporary state of mind. And I couldn't help but think that both laughter and light-heartedness would be scarce from that moment, far into our tenuous future.*

Noah replied, "I was told that we only had two more weeks left before the rain storms begin, and that we have to finish outfitting the interior and complete any remaining exterior work on the ark before that time. In addition, we have to see that everyone and everything is loaded prior to its onset."

"Why is that?" I asked. "Couldn't we work in the rain for a while?"

"Apparently not. Once it starts, there will be no let up, and soon the ground everywhere will become too boggy, even if it isn't completely covered with standing water. The intensity of the rainfall will be beyond anything we've ever experienced or imagined. Plus, it would be a major health hazard for everyone if we track mud and moisture into the far interior of the ark. It has to remain as dry as possible from here on until the end of the voyage. Our survival depends on that. And I'm sure that the fact we've had no rainfall since we started this project was no coincidence."

I asked, with growing hesitation and building anxiety, "So then, what do you want me to do?" *Already, I was being filled with a dread of paralyzing proportions.*

"First off, you'll need to go immediately to the five resettlement areas, find and request that the five members of your Arrival/Settling in Prior to Sailing Committee come with you and meet with me and Ham in three hours. We have to finalize our preparations and assign the tasks that still need to be completed. Then you need to alert everyone through your Messengers and Guardians that all of us, and I mean all of us, have to meet here in this area today at 4 p.m. for our Third Update Meeting. Due to our having to do this, we will leave most of the perimeter of our property unguarded during that meeting. That's because I want everyone within hearing distance of my voice for this convocation. And at this meeting I will brief everyone on what I have recently been told, along with what we've decided needs to be done during this upcoming Committee meeting later this morning. We haven't yet; and we mustn't, henceforth, waste a moment of time before the rain storm begins. Now, hurry, be off, and meet me back here in three hours."

Quickly, I scampered off, not following my very predictable pattern of walking the property's perimeter. *Often Lewis or Lois would follow along with me, and we'd chat and reminisce about the 'good ole days'. About now, I had the feeling we were going to have a lot more time to do just that, trying not to forget that there had been better times than what we were about to experience on this boat trip and well beyond.*

It didn't take me long to find Millie, Todd, Patience, Ian and Fern. Amongst themselves that group chose Millie, the Australian magpie, as the Chair for the Committee. I thought it was a fine choice. Even if she was a bit of a romantic, she had a sound head on her and always seemed to be able to summarize any discussion ably and succinctly. Plus, she had a wonderful singing voice. When she began her early morning or late evening warbling, Holly and I would lapse into the deepest reverie.

And happily we all worked well with Ham, Noah's son. He was an intelligent fellow. Not full of himself, like so many humans seemed to be in those times.

The tendency for so many of them to feel self-important just drove me crazy. What's to feel so important about? Look around you. The real beauty, grace and wonder is in what you see, not what you are. The night sky, filled with stars. The day, filled with sunshine, colors of every description, countless living things of all sizes and shapes. Trees so tall you can hardly see the tops of them, ones it took hundreds of years to grow.

Ham seemed to have a sense of proportion and a recognition of his modest role in what was taking place and in what was to come. And we on the Committee sensed that, and we trusted him.

Millie called our Committee meeting to order at 9 a.m. Just prior to my coming to this meeting, I returned to our home and told Holly what Noah had updated me on and the errand he had me run. Before I left for the meeting, she suggested that it was probably time for me to again begin shouldering my symbol of authority, the shepherd's staff. It was, in her words, time to get "more formal". Discipline, formality and structure were going to have to be uppermost in everyone's minds if these last days of preparation and this voyage were going to be successful. After briefly considering her suggestion, I agreed. And from that moment on, until our debarkation, no one saw me in public without it.

The meeting itself was more or less a rubber stamp of work done earlier, at least in some respects. As a Committee, we had already discussed in great detail the issues that we were assigned. It was now more a matter of everyone on it getting the latest news from Noah and then voting on our final conclusions. Taking them from the top, the following, numbered paragraphs are what we decided and why. Much of the upcoming voyage was hugely impacted by our motley and modest group.

1. As to who would finally travel on the boat, it became crystal clear to each of us, after we saw the mass of animals and birds that had just descended on Nora and Noah's place, and after reexamining the interior of our ninety-nine percent finished boat, that only one pair of all the creatures, feathered and otherwise, could board it. There were to be no exceptions, despite "The Instructions" to have seven pairs of "clean" animals as well. The only exception was for Noah's family members; and that was primarily due to the nature of humans, as all of us had witnessed time and again. They were a warlike lot. Unlike the rest of us, some of them seemed to delight in killing their own kind. Despite that, it was agreed by everyone on the

Committee that the only chance humans had of surviving after the flood waters receded was for them to have multiple family units from the start of the **Second Beginning**. And certainly we all hoped that the behavior and past violence perpetrated by them as a species would end after The Flood. Only time would tell.

The next issue facing us after making this momentous decision was how to inform everyone. It was decided that Noah had to break the news in the meeting later today. Each distinct cluster of birds and animals would then need to select, amongst themselves, who their representative pair would be that would board the boat in two weeks. Whether the remaining six pair stayed on at Noah's would be entirely up to them. If possible, we hoped many would stay to help with the remaining construction, preparations and perimeter security.

The security issue was increasingly becoming more vexing. By now, there were lines of onlookers three and four deep along the entire mile that fronted Nora and Noah's farm. I estimated the number to be well over 5,000 people who were there throughout any given day. And I knew it was only a matter of time before they would sweep across that fence line, even with the Guardians providing protection.

2. Food and other supplies had to be loaded onto the boat immediately. We had no idea when the rain would actually start. Spoilage would be a disaster if any of that material got damp or soaked during the transfer. Bins and shelves were being built in the storage area as we were meeting. It was

decided that we would have a chain of animals that could pass these items, one to the other, from the barns, up the just completed ramp, and down into the hold of the boat. We hoped it would only take a week to transfer all the dried vegetables, fruit, fish, leathers, jerky, seeds, grass cuttings and large, glaze-covered, ceramic jars of drinking water, corn, rice and flour. After all this was loaded, there would then be a cafeteria-style counter built, behind which all the foodstuffs would be stored. [ed. note: See, I bet you thought this form of food service was something new.] Building it adjacent to the storage area meant that everyone had to either go down there or send someone to get their rations of food and water. It was the only practical way we could think of managing to feed everyone on board.

3. The interior of the boat also had to have the living quarters finished, which for the animals and birds consisted of having poles of various diameters for roosts strung across its one hundred foot width at varying heights. Along with them, there would have to be five tree trunks, with their branches still attached, installed in each of the five regional areas. In or on these two accommodations, many of the birds and animals would spend much of their time sleeping, chatting, or singing. And as a last minute suggestion, it was decided that given the ferocity of the predicted rainfall Noah intimated would occur, that a tent-like structure, with a wooden roof, would be erected from the exterior ramp opening on the top deck, extending over to the restroom facilities. Depending on how long the rain lasted, it would at least prevent tracking moisture

back and forth into the interior of the boat. Dryness was right up there next to holiness in our minds.

4. Rules of Conduct were kept to a minimum, at least at this stage. We anticipated that there would be more, once we were afloat and had spent some time together. After all, this was a first. Who could predict everything that was going to happen ahead of time? Basically, we decided to limit the rules to the general admonition that everyone treats each other with respect. There was to be no arguing, fighting, spitting or throwing food. Using the restroom facilities was of paramount importance. If someone had a case of "Montezuma's Revenge", [ed. note: See what I mean about how so much was readily described well before so-called, recorded history?] they'd have to sleep topside until it subsided. Besides, trekking up and down the ramp would keep all of us in shape for the day we would have to forage again on our own.

There were to be only two food distributions a day: a light breakfast and a late afternoon meal. Water would be rationed according to one's size.

In addition, no one under any circumstances was to mess with the candles and oil lamps. They were to be Noah's family's responsibilities to tend to. At all costs we had to prevent a fire on board the boat. With all the pitch inside it, there would be no chance of survival if we had one. All those kinds of supplies were to be kept in the families' quarters.

And finally, there was not going to be any bedding provided for anyone. It would be impossible to keep the areas clean if there was straw, leaves or grasses to sleep on. It was time for everyone to "cowboy up". [ed. note: uh huh..., even cowboys are timeless.]

With all this agreed upon and then voted on unanimously to present to the audience later that day, we disbanded and awaited the large meeting to come. I then took the opportunity to walk the perimeter of the property and explore the five regional areas of wildlife. It was all a marvel. There was no fighting or menacing sounds. There was just the low murmur of living creatures knowing that something of lasting significance was about to happen and not being sure their role in any of it. They were a grand lot, and I was proud to be part of them. Say what you will, we animals and birds are a credit to this world. Without us, it would be a much sadder and more gruesome place. By noon, I arrived back home and ate lunch with Holly. We decided to rest afterwards until the 4 p.m. meeting started. I needed to. All the mornings' decisions had made me quite nervous, knowing what was ahead for so many of these brave and wonderful newcomers.

Come 3:30 that same afternoon, after a short nap, Holly and I walked down our hill to the area where a crowd was assembling. There already were hundreds of birds perched on stumps and the just-finished railing on the top deck of the boat. Along with them, there were even more animals dotting the area, sitting or standing in small groups. The forested area east of the boat had been cleared for acres. Even the branches had been piled in huge mounds and were later burned. There was concern that with the flooding, that they could form a barrier or clog the passageway for the boat once it began to float. The ramp was also on the east side of the boat, which prevented the public from seeing at least some of the loading and stocking of supplies. The effort had been made to do most of that during the nighttime. During the day that material was to be sorted and stacked ready to carry over to the boat at nightfall.

And as we entered the assembly area, for the first time I was struck by the immensity of the ark, as Noah called it. Throughout its being built, I pretty much looked the other way. It reminded me too much of the horrors that would befall so very many. But at that moment, I was stunned by the sheer accomplishment and size of it. Standing alongside one of the keel cants, it, in itself, was almost taller than I was. And looking up the sixty feet-plus of its height was dizzying. The dark brown bark exterior gave you the sense it was almost alive, that the trees were still growing, but without branches. It had an eerie quality, almost other-worldly. You expected it to expand outward, as if taking a deep breath or about to sigh, as it contemplated the reason it was built.

The expanse of stumpage extended out to the boat's side and away for hundreds of feet. The birds and animals, however, were mostly concentrated in its shadow. Everyone was aware of not wanting to alarm the public any more than they already were. And by 3:55 p.m., Noah and his family walked around the south side of the boat. While some of them sat or stood with the rest of us,

Noah strode briskly up the ramp until he stood at its upper edge on the top deck and then turned to face all of us.

The ramp was built of two large one hundred foot long beams, each debarked and limbed to make them easier to slide up onto the top deck. One side had been hewed level for the twelve foot long planks to be attached to them. On top of the planks, approximately every twelve inches lath boards were attached to prevent anyone from slipping. At its top underside, a twelve foot long cant was attached to hook over the top edge of the upper deck and lock the ramp in place when loading or unloading. The same was done at the bottom to anchor the ramp, and also for both cants to provide the extra bracing needed to wedge the ramp between the boat's upper deck's gunwales when it was skidded up onto the top deck. We couldn't have it slip off mid-voyage. There would have been no safe way for us to safely exit the boat, if it somehow slid overboard.

Come 4 p.m. sharp, Noah then looked out and must have been humbled to see before him the mass of life, quietly waiting for him to speak. By that moment, the railing on the east side of the boat was filled with birds, as was two hundred feet of space from the boat into the once forested area.

"Welcome, newcomers to our farm," Noah called out in his loudest, booming voice. "Nora, my family and I are both humbled and so relieved to see all of you here today. The reason you came all this distance is beyond my ability to describe or comprehend, but you took it upon yourselves to trust us and many of you have traveled for months to get here. I only wish that some of what I have to say today would be a comfort to all of you, but it won't be."

And from that point, he immediately began to tell the audience what our Committee had discussed and decided earlier that morning, leaving to the last the part about only one pair of each of us being able to board and travel. He went on to say he hoped everyone who would not be traveling on the ark in two weeks would not decide to leave immediately, but he understood if they did. He did not ask for a show of how many might stay. Instead, he requested that each of the seven pairs quietly regroup after this meeting and decide amongst themselves who would be the selected pair to sail.

Once it was decided who that pair was, they were to inform me, which came as a complete surprise. I had thought that my work days were over, but this directive was only the beginning of the chores that Noah had planned for me as our voyage progressed.

And it is incumbent on me to note at this time that the process of choosing who went and who stayed was decided by the thousands of species that evening without a hitch. It was nothing short of miraculous. Essentially, among the pairs chosen, they also included all of the Guardians, Messengers and Committee members. And that included Holly and I. But as I later thought about it, it typified the overall character of animals and birds everywhere. We are used to seeing and experiencing life as a journey, one that could end suddenly and without apparent reason. As a consequence, we value each moment and condition ourselves to make hard decisions without complaint. Sudden death, hunger, thirst, freezing temperatures or unbearable heat, none of these are uncommon in our own or our families' lives. We have become disciplined to accept the unexpected, to actually expect it. And we take the greatest pleasure in each day we are given. Sensing that life throughout the world is about to experience a disappearance or extinction event, unlike what it has undergone in previous times, we were all simply relieved that at least some us had the opportunity to live on.

This was to be in stark contrast to what happened two weeks later with the humans who had been gathering daily at the fence line.

As a species, at least those outside Nora, Noah and their family, they seem determined to be ungraceful, petty and angry so much of the time. It's a shame. The sheer beauty of life around each of us should keep them in constant awe and gratitude to at least have been privileged enough to witness it, even if it was for only a brief time. I only hoped that whoever came after Noah and his family would be more mature and understanding of their place in this magnificent world. I guessed only time would tell.

Anyway, Noah concluded his hour long speech with a simple prayer, the first I ever heard him pray. And in it, he asked for the strength and courage to see that day through and the many to follow. But it was not a prayer just for him and his family; it was for all of us! He actually prayed for us birds and animals as well. That really impressed me!!

My feeling was that humans thought of us as godless and unfeeling, unknowing and unworthy. [ed. note: You may want to reread in The Good Book where the Creator made all of us animals and fowl, and then said it was "good". Saying so might lead you to believe we weren't all that "bad" and might even warrant a portion of plaintive prayers Noah uttered that day. At least that's my editorial opinion.]

When he concluded his prayer, I looked over at Holly and saw that there were tears in her eyes. She, too, was touched by his recognition and acknowledgement of us. We actually counted for something. We weren't to be used, killed, stuffed, eaten, or simply be the objects of sport and folly. We mattered, and we had helped make his and his family's survival a possibility in the days, weeks, months and years ahead.

To celebrate this acknowledgement, I found out later that Lolly called together a very special group of her fellow birds and asked Lance and them to begin a tradition that lasted from that same night, until we each departed Noah's ark so many months later.

And from that night forward, this small band of songsters collected one-by-one on either the boat's top railing, as they did that first night, or during the downpour on the railing surrounding the entranceway ramp down into the boat, now covered by the Ramp House and the attached tents extending over to the Restroom Facilities, and sang their lungs out for one hour straight. The musical composition of this group included the haunting call of the loon, the melodious warbling of the Australian magpie and a few North American songbirds, the soul-stirring echoes of the Western meadowlark and two of his cousins found worldwide, the dazzling trilling of the mockingbird, the chiming of the bell minor and the unnerving, barely audible whispers of the whippoorwill. It was a chorus like no other, before or since. Their music that night comforted and calmed all who heard it, as it echoed throughout that valley.

Appropriately enough, thanks to Lance's suggestion, there was also a welcoming voice to awaken us each morning thereafter, as well. He enlisted Kyle and his mate to perform their unmatchable wakeup calls the next morning. Their laughter gave us as great a lift each morning, just as the evening chorus provided us comforting reassurance each night.

I always felt forever indebted to Lance and Lolly for their thoughtfulness and dedication to provide all of us reveille and taps each day and evening. It served to bring us all closer together day by day. And in the horror that was about to befall our world, that was no small matter. Somehow, in all of this, we had to be reassured, in a very tangible way, that there was a **Creator** who still loved us and not just a **Floodmaster** who was angry and weary of us all.

ELEVEN: THE RIOT AND THE RAIN

Almost wordlessly for everyone, our labors for the next two weeks proceeded at a frantic pace. Very few non-boarding animals or birds left Nora and Noah's, at least not until the supplies were all loaded. The twelve foot wide ramp allowed the passage of traffic each direction and hastened the final building and loading. And by loading under the cover of darkness, it kept the public curiosity at a minimum, or so we hoped. Still, with each dawn, there were now thousands upon thousands of bystanders, watching every move we made. And with the increased ground shaking, the public had grown more impatient and agitated since that initial attempt by a few of them to invade our building site. By now, Lois and Lewis had to keep the front fence line almost fully staffed with Guardians. No gaps were possible, given the tendency now for onlookers to try and sneak through. The situation was becoming untenable, and Noah sensed it.

Because of his concerns, come sunset the thirteenth day, just before the final two weeks of dry weather ended and after all the supplies were loaded, we secured and reinforced the tenting that extended from the Ramp House to the Restroom Facilities with wood framing and large rocks. And then it was quietly announced to everyone that our jobs were finished.

The interior of Noah's ark had been completed two days previous to that evening. All the food and other supplies were stored in stalls, shelves and cupboards on the lower deck. A cafeteria-style serving counter had been built in front of them. Along with it, long tables, some with benches, were built and installed in that same area for everyone to use. All food had to be consumed in that area. There were to be no exceptions. Likewise, the various roosts and lairs were now all installed.

All that done, to finalize all this work, Nora and Noah and their family members began thanking and embracing the hundreds and thousands of birds and animals who were not taking the voyage but who had made it all possible. After each embrace, each was told they could leave, knowing they had made life's future existence in this world somewhat more likely in the days to come. And, almost without exception, the mass of animals and birdlife left that night for the Delta region, to rejoin their kin and spend the remaining time left for each with their loved ones.

Afterwards, Noah announced to the rest of us who would be climbing up into the boat one last time that next morning, to be there and boarded by 7 a.m. sharp. He emphasized that the ramp had to be secured on the top deck and all of us inside the ark by 8 a.m.

Again, as was the custom for Holly and me, and now with our extended family, we all huddled together and talked far into that fateful, thirteenth night. It was the least we could do, given the outcome of our being chosen as the pair to join Noah on his ark.

For all of us, including every animal and bird who ascended the ramp or flew onto its top deck that next morning, it always remained just a boat. "Ark" sounded too grand, somehow. Too special. Too privileged. It possessed nothing of that mystery or quality to any of us. It was simply a very large boat or floating box. It was the cargo that was so priceless. And spending that last night with family and close friends imbedded that conviction in us for the remainder of our lives.

I have no idea when Holly and I actually were able to fall asleep, but I know exactly when we awoke. It was 6:55 a.m. the next morning!!

Screaming at the top of my scratchy voice, I bolted upright and shook Holly, "Holly!! We're late!! We're very late!!! We must run as fast as we can!! Wake UP! HURRY!! GO!! GO... GO!!"

Bounding out of our burrow, with her in the lead, I got about 50 feet away and remembered. Calling out to her, as she picked up speed racing downhill, "I forgot my staff!! I must go back and get it!! I'll follow you. GO ON, HURRY!!"

It is still a blur, but somehow I returned, grabbed my "Merrill's hook", as everyone was now calling it, tucked it under my belt once I got outside again and began running as fast as I ever remembered doing. It was all I could do to keep from tripping and beginning a catastrophic tumbling down the steep hill.

As soon as I could focus long enough to see what lay before me, my fear and horror elevated to sheer, absolute panic and near paralysis. Because of the need to have everyone climb up the ramp by 7 a.m., the front of Nora and Noah's property was now completely unguarded, and the people who had gathered there day in and day out for the last 28 weeks were now climbing the fences or knocking them down. Thousands were now surging forward toward the massive boat. There was nothing to stop them.

Some were holding what looked like clubs, others had spears and all of them looked fierce and determined. It was like their having to stand and just look for all these weeks had incensed them so much that only a violent and destructive response would compensate for their being kept away. It was obvious to me at that moment that my life and possibly everyone else's on that boat were in extreme peril. All this work, planning, heart-wrenching decision-making and possibly, even hope, was going to be dashed in a matter of minutes or hours. But somehow I kept up my pace and the ramp appeared to come closer and closer.

I could see that Holly had already been swept up on it by Lois, who with Lewis were the sole crewmembers left at the end of the ramp. And Lois was hurriedly ushering Holly up the ramp to safety on the top deck. Or at least she hoped she could. I doubted she knew entirely what I was seeing racing toward them. As I flew up onto the ramp, it was obvious that Noah had given the order to start raising it. It was now 7 a.m.

By the time I reached the base of the ramp, it was already three feet off the ground; and I couldn't jump up to reach it!

Lewis, still at its leading edge, called out to me, "Extend that staff toward me, hook end first!! Hurry! DO IT!!"

And with a maneuver any master juggler would have admired, I slipped it out of my belt, enough distance so that Lewis could swing out one of his front paws with claws fully extended and catch the curved portion of my staff.

"Hold on tight, Merrill!!" he yelled. "I'm going to give you a yank!"

And yank he did. The staff and I were swung up into the air and onto the ramp about ten feet above him. He lofted me like I weighed only ounces. Then he yelled, "RUN, Merrill! RUN AS FAST AS YOU CAN!! And I'll be right behind you! We have no time to waste!"

As I got to the top of the sliding ramp, I saw a most remarkable sight. Sometime during the last two weeks, thick reinforced rope and leather loops had been attached to the end of the ramp and along both sides of it. At the front were Elliot and Elaine, the two hippos and the two rhinos attached to those loops and straining with all their strength. Then along one side were Perry and his mate, plus two grizzly bears, two polar bears and two brown bears. On the other side were Olive, Graham and their mates and two bison. All of them were straining at their utmost limit to get the ramp onto the top deck as quickly as possible. When the crew at the front end could no longer pull, as it approached the other side of the boat, they quickly removed the ropes and harnesses and helped nudge the ramp in between the two sides of the boat. Within a matter of minutes it was fully raised and secured in place. And Lewis and I were able to rejoined Lois and Holly safely and unharmed.

But below us the riot only intensified. To everyone's credit, over the last month or so, it had been a strict rule that any rocks, stones or large pieces of wood had to be carried far away from the building site. It was a precaution that we all felt was necessary, given the anger we saw mounting with the onlookers in front of the property. But that didn't stop the out of control mob from beginning to beat on the side of the boat with their clubs and spears. Some began to throw them up at us, but the height made it impossible for most of them to reach the top deck. But as everyone was being ushered under the tent and into the ramp-way leading to the interior of the boat, the few of us left topside noticed that there were ominous activities going on at various points around the base of the keel. People were gathering the wood shavings and preparing to light fires. They were going to build a huge funeral pyre! I began yelling to Noah what I was seeing, but he had raced into the Wheel House for a moment, to do what I could only guess. As it turned out, it was to pray.

Because it was at that moment that two things happened that forever changed this world and all its inhabitants. First, the ground began to shake violently, as it had been doing throughout the planet, elsewhere, for months. And most importantly, clouds began to move over the horizon toward us. But these were not any ordinary clouds. They were like none any of us who had been isolated at Noah's or at the Delta had ever seen. But the passengers who had come from afar, from along all the coastlines, they knew. These were the clouds they had fearfully observed forming for months.

Steadily, as we watched in open-mouthed amazement, the cloudy mass surged forth. These were no puffy, introductory clouds that you usually see preceding a storm front; some white, some grey and all of them colorfully mixed in front of an azure blue sky. It was a massive wave of total blackness, extending as high upward as you could see. And with them were the sounds of rolling thunder; its intensity alone caused the ground to shake and your teeth to rattle. All the noise building around us became absolutely terrifying.

And below us, the uncontrollable riot was caught completely off-guard by the storm front and the earth movements. A few had started their fires and were looking for branches to fuel them and to get the underside of our boat ablaze. But then the winds came. Gales like none you could imagine. I knew the tenting would be torn to pieces, but the winds, for some reason, were not as strong on the top deck as those you could see around us. A sheltered calm seemed to prevail on the boat itself. But below us, and beyond, the winds were mounting by the second. It scattered most of the fires and their makers. But a few persisted.

Then 8 a.m., February 17, arrived; and the first drops of rain began to fall. [ed. note: See accompanying Appendix, Genesis 7:11.]   Noah turned to each of us and said it was time to leave the area and go below. The time had come. The earth was now about to be baptized and cleansed. Our journey was about to begin. And by the time we were all under cover, the rain began to pound the upper deck.   It was good that Ham thought additional wood supports and roofing was needed over the tenting. Otherwise, all of it would have collapsed under the torrent that followed for the next forty days and nights.

I was the last one to get a glimpse of the area around the boat before everyone was ushered into its hold.   And what I saw caused me such almost unbearable distress; and it still does. It was the sight of people streaming away from the boat, screaming and thrashing their arms. Many were falling down, as the ground became so slippery, so quickly.   Others were looking skyward, as the darkness enveloped them, with their mouths open in screams of disbelief and horror.   I knew I was watching the end of life, or at least any which was beyond this ark of Noah's.

THE VOYAGE

TWELVE: THE SHAKE DOWN

In all the confusion and noise that surrounded everyone's mad rush to get further onto the interior ramps or, for us who were the last ones off the top deck, to get at least under the Ramp House roof, any semblance of order was lost. It was sheer, terrifying pandemonium. Shouts, directives, cautions, pleas and wailing were all mixed together in what had to be an appropriate, even measured, if you will, response to what was beginning to take place outside our wooden shelter. At least we weren't crushing each other in a stampede for safety or seeking quiet from the awful din outside. The volume and sheer pitch of the storm raging around us sounded as if all the heavens were shouting, in almost uncontrollable rage, at our world. It wasn't hard to believe at that moment that all life was indeed about to be swept from the face of Pangaea.

And then above the roaring outside and the near-hysteria inside the boat's entranceway, I heard the powerful voice of Noah again. "MERRILL!!!"

he shouted, "GET YOUR VOYAGE ISSUES'
COMMITTEE TOGETHER AND BOTH YOU
AND THEM JOIN NORA, SHEM AND I IN THE
WHEEL HOUSE IN FIFTEEN MINUTES!!... DO
YOU HEAR ME?!! he then yelled, as if seeking
confirmation.

"Yeah, chief, I do." I replied with much less
forcefulness. "I do, because I'm parked right at
your feet; just look down, and you'll see me."

"Oh, sorry," he noted with some surprise. "I
thought you'd gotten swept down the ramps into the
far interior of the ark. Anyway, we need to meet
right away. There are agenda items that we now
have to address, that we couldn't before. Honestly,
I wasn't sure this venture would ever even get this
far along. All this confusion and noise is as big a
surprise to me as it must be to everyone else in here.
And try to calm everyone you pass or see along the
way, will you?"

"Sure thing, boss," I answered, knowing that
he had to be under a lot of pressure and highly
stressed at this moment. "We'll get everyone under
control soon enough. It's has to be the shock of
what is happening, and then there's that confounded
noise outside that's got everyone, including me,
upset and so frightened. I'll get everyone to meet
you in fifteen minutes, just as you ask."

And after that brief exchange, it took me ten
minutes to weave my way along the ramps and in
and out of the deck areas to locate Glenda, Carl,
Olive, Paula and Graham. [ed. note: See the
accompanying Appendix: "VOYAGE
COMMITTEE MEMBERS"] Olive and Graham

were still exhausted from the strenuous effort necessary to pull the ramp up onto the top deck. They were huddled together with their partners on the second deck, the one reserved for the larger animals. All of them easily topped the two hundred pound inclusion weight. Carl and Paula, on the other hand, were perched on the railing at the far end of the Ramp House and had heard every word that Noah had shouted at me. They just looked at me and nodded, then shrugged. *I never met two more unflappable critters in my life.* But to find Glenda I had to wiggle and squirm my way down the ramps to the third deck's bow section, where she was already curling up, ready to take a nap.

I swear, what calm that gal had. They needed to give everyone an injection of whatever it was that was circulating through her veins. It was unnerving to me to see how calmly she took everything that happened around her. This particular Committee was going to be the balm I needed to keep my own emotions in check: they and Holly.

I likewise found Holly on the third deck's bow section. And wouldn't you know, she was also starting to curl up for a nap, having been awakened so abruptly by me to make our desperate dash to the madhouse earlier that morning.

"Why was I the only one of the small group who was so emotionally strung out?" I wondered aloud. *I hoped this voyage would give me some of their courage and calm in the face of danger. But deep within me, I doubted that was possible.*

Having quickly found my Committee

members, this allowed me a few minutes to spend with Holly and settle down, somewhat, myself. She informed me that she wanted to rest before the first meal was prepared and served to everyone. It was going to be delayed today until 1 p.m., due to the meeting we were about to have and also to give everyone a chance to recover some of their composure. Besides, it was obvious no one would be so hungry that they'd need to eat any time soon, after what we had experienced and were experiencing.

That aside, it was such a great comfort for me to just lay down briefly with her. Without her reassuring presence throughout these last 28 weeks, I would not have had the courage or will to follow any of Noah's instructions. I would have just buried myself deeper into a burrow in complete isolation. Much of what had been accomplished in this timeframe, directly and indirectly, had to be credited to her.

Somewhat rested and relieved, I soon rose and began to leave her slipping into a sound sleep, but as I rolled over onto my feet, she muttered, "Don't forget your staff. You needed it awhile ago, and it will serve you well throughout this voyage. Take it with you always, dear, and I'll see you later."

Working my way back up the ramps to the top deck wasn't quite the chore it had been coming down them. Gradually, everyone was making their way into their assigned areas and collapsing in fright and despair. There was no sense of being part of a job well done or of being on the most prized list of chosen individuals on the planet. No one felt special. Everyone was despondent.

But Noah's call to reassemble our Committee gave a few of us at least a diversion from our desperate thoughts for the immediate future. We all believed that this venture was absolutely going to be a minute-to-minute struggle for survival. Joy and relief were not emotions anyone of us experienced during most of this boat ride. And in part that was out of homage to those family members and so many others that were to be lost over the next days and months.

Within the fifteen minutes allotted the Committee, the nine of us eventually assembled and huddled together at the ramp entrance on the top deck. Noah then warned us that outside our Ramp House cover, it was gusting and raining far beyond anything any of us had ever experienced. He recommended that we follow him to the Wheel House, running as fast as we could without falling. Once there, he had already set aside some blankets earlier that morning for each of us to use for drying off. The same was to be the case when we ran back here after our meeting was over. This was to be the standard procedure for the next forty days and nights. And at his mark, we each ducked under the flapping tent side, and ran frantically over to our meeting room, the Wheel House.

After everyone had reassembled there and dried off, we anxiously sat on the chairs and benches scattered throughout the room. Pulling them together, we initially huddled together around the room's one table for warmth, sitting in total silence, listening to the howling around us. The one, forward-facing window in the Wheel House was framed somewhat like a square porthole; and by that I mean it was recessed into the log framing. For added protection, it had an outside overhang to prevent most of the rain from beating in. But in preparation for the torrential rainfall, its wooden shutters were also closed, so the room was dry and snug but that left us unable to see beyond the structure's four walls.

At that moment, the rain was so hard, it sounded like a river rushing down on top of your head. Never, and I mean never, had any of us experienced a storm like this one. And it wasn't until much later that we had any idea of the amount of rain that was falling upon us...and everywhere else throughout Pangaea.

To give you some idea what I am trying to describe, at the end of our voyage we used the following observations to calculate what the actual rainfall amount was that day and the next thirty-nine to follow. Allowing for the fact that every prominence, including the highest in our world at that time, was to be covered with water once this massive storm had ended, we used Mt. Ararat as the point of reference. Based upon our measurements, after we finally moored on one of its ledges some five months later, we determined that its height was close to 13,680 feet. Don't think about wanting to ask me how we determined that now. We just did. And furthermore, given that forty days and nights has 960 hours, we calculated that if you divided that total number of hours into 13,800 feet, you got the average rainfall it took to cover EVERYTHING, including Mt. Ararat. That amount came to be a staggering fourteen feet, three-quarter inches of rain per hour!!! And that was the amount we were hearing, thundering down upon us at the time of our first Committee meeting.

(I know, I know. If anyone is reading this…ever…you're thinking, that can't be! Well, do the math yourself and see. And believe me, it was a sight and sound to behold as it was happening. And worse still, as it turned out, I was going to be the only live body on board this bark-covered-excuse-for-a-boat who had to be out in the Wheel House every, single day for the next 189 days. And now let me explain why.

Noah called the meeting to order and said another one of his prayers, which I must admit were becoming more and more comforting. It wasn't clear to me at the time **Who** he was addressing, but simply hearing Noah's voice, one that was not panicked and whining was reassuring, no matter **Who** was being addressed.

Then he followed up with, "Folks, we have some urgent business to attend to. While I realize what is happening outside this Wheel House is far beyond anything any of us could have imagined or wanted to, we must forge on. Every life on this ark depends on it.

"I will start with the most straightforward issue first, that of the bits of colored yarn you see in the wooden boxes in the far corner. After this morning's meeting, we need to see that they are issued to the respective groups in each of the deck areas. Particularly for the first few days or weeks, if not for the entire voyage, we need to know who is quartered where. They are to be tied loosely around the necks of every animal and bird on the ark, including you here. And, as a review, we are to issue the white ones to the largest animals and a few birds, berthed on the second deck. Red ones belong to the African contingent, blue ones are for those from Australia, green for North/South America, yellow for Europe and orange for Asia. Please see that everyone is wearing one by tomorrow morning.

"Next, we need to assign a certain number of the ark's passengers to "watch" duty and discuss what they shall be doing. This may come as some surprise to you, but Shem, Nora and I felt it was necessary for the welfare and safety of the ark. At all times there needs to be someone on duty in this Wheel House, the 'Control Center' of this ship. There will be three eight-hour shifts each day. The first watch starts at 12 a.m. and lasts until 8 a.m. The second watch of the day is from 8 a.m. to 4 p.m., and the third one is from 4 p.m. to midnight. There will be thirty-six of us who will be responsible for this duty, which means that each of us will rotate through a cycle every twelve days. Except for Merrill. He will have to come back here every morning for report at 8 a.m., as will I at least for the foreseeable future. And immediately thereafter, he will prepare the log for what occurred on the previous three watches that day. I will hand out the assigned days and shifts at the end of this meeting. [See the accompanying Appendix: "THE ARK'S 'WATCH' ASSIGNMENTS".]

"And finally, I need to discuss with you what it is that you will need to remember and then pass on to the one relieving you, until Merrill has a chance to hear the twenty-four hour days' full report. Essentially, each of us needs to keep track of the ark's condition, any weather-related issues or other problems and unusual happenings that occurred during your shift.

"Merrill will then record all this. And 'why Merrill?' you ask; because it is he and Holly who are the only ones who know how to write. I'm too old to learn, and neither of them have had the time to teach anyone else. We are privileged to have them on board this vessel. They, to my knowledge, are the only ones on this world that know how, and they were the first to devise this technique. They call it 'Pre-Cuneiform' writing. Where they got that term I'll never guess, but who's to argue. [ed note: See the accompanying Appendix: "CUNEIFORM ALPHABET AND THE EARLIEST NUMBERS", and be amazed! Much more began, occurred and ended with that flooding than was previously known. Uppermost in my mind was what happened to the ability of animals and birds to speak? Why did that disappear after Noah's ark landed and the new generations of creatures began to populate the planet? Maybe that's also the first example of the Law of Unintended Consequences.]

"What Merrill will do each day is use the caulk that is piled in that big box at the other end of this room and write down what you report to him each morning at 8 a.m. He will mark-off sections on all the walls in here, each section representing one day; and he will continue to do this until this voyage has ended. Then after our final departure and relocation, he and Holly will transfer the information written on these walls onto clay tablets or some other object that will be a permanent record of this trip and the events leading up to it."

It was at this point that the Wheel House was filled with an immense gasp…from me!

I had never been told anything about this! Furthermore, I had never told anyone about this ability. It was something Holly and I did in our spare time. SHE must have said something to Nora or Noah! The whole aspect of it all made me feel weak and ill. This meant that Holly and I would not be leaving this dratted boat anytime soon after the flood waters receded. In fact, it looked like it might be our future home forever!!…

Noah concluded the meeting with a request that everyone quickly return to their family member below deck, as well as asking each of the five committee members to go to the back of the room and pick out the colored yarn which corresponded to their region of origin, and then hand them out to all the animals and birds they represented. Likewise, he asked Shem to take a considerable number of each colored yarn and pass them out to the residents in the large animal and bird compound on Deck #2. And with that, sensing my shock and seeing my dejected appearance, he turned to me and asked that I stay behind for a moment after the other Committee members leave.

Wordlessly, against the background of the ferocious storm raging outside the Wheel House, while Noah braced the door open, each fled into The Rage, as we began to call it, making their way back to the Ramp House and to safety.

Noah then closed the door, turned to me and asked, "Are you going to be ok with all this? I know I have already burdened you with a lot of duties and responsibilities. Nora and I are so thankful you and Holly have been here to help with all this. And I know I haven't been able to keep up with all the ark building instructions I was initially given by the **Lord**. We were supposed to have the ark built in seven days… There was no way. And I'm sure that delay has led to the increased violence we are now witnessing with this storm. It was becoming more pent-up and violent on the shorelines of the world during this delay. And we weren't able to get pitch around all the outside of the ark until the last minute, due to the need for more pitch than we initially estimated we would need. I hope it was enough to prevent leakage. With the amount of rainfall and hardly enough time for the pitch to harden, I worry we could spring leaks so severe that this hulk never gets off the ground and we all drown on or in it. And then I'm now worried about you. What do you say?"

"I don't know what to say, boss," I remember I replied. "Probably keeping busy will help Holly and I cope with all this, but I fear I will let you down. It's not like what I do is that great. We write in a kind of shorthand. But maybe with practice I can gain the ability to express myself more completely. Obviously, this venture from the onset to the final docking of this boat needs to be recorded, if possible. I just hope Holly, Nora or you are always with me to do the final processing and inscribing. Otherwise, I can't guarantee anything much will come of what you have asked me to do."

"I'm sure some of us will be there," Noah reassured me. "At least we will be, if this massive hunk of wood stays together and doesn't sink."

And it was just at that minute, approximately two and half hours after the rain had begun, that we felt the first lunge and shifting of the vessel. With these, there were massive moans and cracking sounds, as if the boat was waking up and stretching after a deep sleep. Then there was a rocking to one side and then the other, pitching both of us off balance. If I hadn't had my staff to steady me, I'm sure I would have fallen. Noah was able to reach out and catch himself against the door jam.

"It's happening!" he shouted. "We're becoming dislodged from our being supported on the ground and are beginning to float! My heavens, it didn't take long at all for that to happen! I thought it would be days before there was enough water around us to give us any buoyancy. [ed. note: See, even Archimedes' Principle of buoyancy was not a new discovery. Even some of the major laws of physics were being toyed with in much earlier times. How smug we became.]

"But to do so, there has to be at least twenty to thirty feet of water surrounding us at this moment. There is no way we could displace the amount of water needed to float otherwise. The amount of rain falling per hour must be unfathomable!"

And as you already know, it was. By my estimation, in the two and half hours since the storm began, there had been over thirty-six feet of rainfall!! And now the fun really began.

"Quick, Merrill," Noah shouted, even though it was just us in the room. "We have to rush over to the living quarters and check for leaks and calm the passengers. They'll all be startled by this sudden movement occurring so soon. We can't let panic take hold, particularly if they begin to see some water seepage. We must hurry! Come on! I'll get Ham to come over here right away to begin the first watch."

Rushing back to the ramp, it was obvious to both of us that Noah's ark was now bouncing wildly side to side, as it became fully buoyant. Once we descended the ramp, the noise inside was deafening. Combining the storm's fury, with the shouts, screams, squawks and roars of everyone being tossed effortlessly to and fro, the boat's interior was filled with a horrifying din. And without thinking or asking Noah if I should, I began rushing from deck to deck, region to region, shouting "DON'T ROCK...THE BOAT!", "DON'T ROCK...THE BOAT!!" It was all I could think to yell. I felt if everyone kept up their uproar and wildly running about, we would surely tip over and capsize. This boat, for all the effort and designing that went into building it, was hardly seaworthy, much less capable of withstanding its load being shifted side to side by stampeding animals and people. I sensed that we would perish within the next few minutes if order was not restored immediately.

Fortunately, there were others who also took up my desperate cry, and with each one who did, it seemed to add more calm to a situation, which was on the brink of total chaos. At least by calling out, there was one less scream or shout, and the chaos gradually subsided. Almost simultaneously with this chorus of cries, the boat, as well, appeared to steady itself.

But don't get me wrong, the scent of fear was overpowering prior to these calls for calm. It wasn't just a matter of feeling it; you could taste it and smell it. Fortunately, however, the interior of the boat also had a heavy fragrance of cut fir and pine wood, mixed with resin and pitch to quickly dissipate that disturbing odor.

As a credit to the work crews, they elected to pitch the inside of the boat first. That gave it more time to season and for the fumes to lessen somewhat before we occupied all the decks. Otherwise, I could imagine the interior atmosphere might have been overwhelming, possibly even toxic.

After I had dashed throughout the boat warning everyone to settle down, I then took the time to tour the lower deck for any breaching problems. It was my first chance to just look around in wonder at what was taking place in all the decks. And a wonder it was.

And luckily, there were no signs of seepage anywhere, throughout the lower fourth deck area. The draft of the boat was not precisely known at that time, but we guessed it had to be somewhere in the neighborhood of fourteen to twenty feet, when you combined all the tonnage of the wooden structure itself, our supplies and the occupants. Whatever it was, for the moment at least, there were no problems associated with water entering the boat. That, in itself, was a miracle.

Remarkably, despite the pandemonium elsewhere, preparations were taking place on the fourth deck for the first onboard meal for everyone. Nora and Holly were orchestrating that effort. The cafeteria-style serving table was covered with a huge red linen table cloth. And on top of it were ceramic bowls of all sizes and descriptions, filled with dried food. Still in progress, were others busy filling pitchers of water and placing them at regular intervals on each table. Water was our drink of choice, as well as it being our only option. Noah's family had some mead and grape wine in their living quarters, both of which they occasionally drank and even offered to Holly and I once in a while during our confinement on board the boat. Bear in mind, this austere menu, at that moment and for the duration of our voyage was meant to sustain, not satiate. And there was no telling if we had stored enough of either. It was a constant worry for everyone. And as a common agreement among us all, it was decided during one of our assembles with everyone in attendance that no one, not one individual, was to be sacrificed to feed someone else. That action alone would have unhinged everyone, releasing pure rage and mutiny that would have undoubtedly gripped the entire boat. It was agreed before anyone boarded this vessel that day; we'd either all survive together or perish together. There were to be no exceptions.

Before I left the supply and cafeteria area that first day, I quickly found Holly and gave her as reassuring a hug as I could muster. We both looked at each other, sensing the other knew that life, at that very moment, was being swept away around us.

It was, for me, the most haunting moment of my life. There was no survivor's elation. It was time for the deepest and most profound mourning. I hoped I could finish my initial tour of the boat, and then I was going to join Holly; and, together, we were going to escape to our small space on the third deck and huddle there until I had to go for the first log report at 8 a.m. the next morning.

Carrying my staff, I next walked over to the stern side of the fourth deck, where the animals and birds of Europe and Asia were encamped. It was a sight beyond belief. Roost poles of different diameters were suspended and extended the entire one hundred foot width of the boat and at different levels. On them were birds of all the sizes and colors imaginable. They were all in pairs. And they were all in full voice. It was no longer the sounds of panic, but of conversation and of a very few beginning to warble songs of lament. Some were flying from one roost to another or down to the deck to converse with a newly made animal friend. Others were just flying to keep their strength up and probably to combat depression and panic. Under and over some of the roosts were a series of simulated trees, with multiple leafless branches crowded with clinging animals of all sorts. The most common were the monkeys and lemurs.

And on the deck were countless varieties of the smaller animals of those two regions. Only the assigned bits of yarn facilitated knowing where they originated from. Each pair had only enough room for themselves with maybe a couple of feet separating them from another pair. Aisles had been drawn by the boat builders once the pitch was set, using caulk to mark off walkways and designated living quarters. The living quarters varied somewhat in square-foot area; it depending entirely upon the size of its occupants. There were sixteen aisles, extended from the ramp to the stern. Each was two feet wide and the living spaces were about four feet wide. The area was overflowing with life. It made my heart ache.

And so it went, as I surveyed the third and second decks. And by the time I arrived on the second deck, there was now a steady flow of birds and animals, walking, running or flying to the top deck's Restroom Facilities at the stern. The ramps, from that moment on, until we escaped confinement months later, were highways, streaming with a never-ending parade of life forms.

There were two areas that probably do need some extra explanation as to what I observed that first day: the large animal section and the area reserved for Nora, Noah, their children and their families.

Upon entering the second deck's large animal and bird compartment, I was immediately struck by the rainbow of colors before me. Because representatives from all five regions were housed there, the red, orange, blue, green and yellow yarn scarves brightened up the oil lamps' dank atmosphere, like none other in the other quarters below us. Around the three walls were two tiers of balconies, each about seven feet above the main deck floor and then above the first balcony. There were ladders leading up to them, oddly placed along their lengths. And with forelegs draped over the front edge of the back side balconies were what seemed to be all of the world's largest cats. Panthers, cheetahs, tigers, cougars, leopards and saber-tooth tigers, all appeared to be lounging unfazed by all that was going on around them. On the port side were the larger primates, including Olive and Graham, both busily conversing with each other while positioned on the end closest to the interior ramps. The starboard side included a mixture of mid-sized animals, including the hyenas, antelopes, and kudus. The deck itself housed emus, ostriches, and other large flightless birds, along with the largest and tallest non-hoofed and hoofed animals, like the bison, rhinos, giraffes and Elliot and Elaine. This last pair was also at the closest edge to the interior ramps. Lewis and Lois were on the other side of the room from Elaine and Elliot. Olive, Graham, Elaine, Lois and their partners were instructed to reside in these particular places because having all four couples being positioned there made it much easier for Noah or I to alert or to summon them for some errand or meeting.

Because Deck #2's floor was reserved for the world's largest creatures, it had also been subdivided with chalk. It was marked off with one ten-foot wide walkway down the middle of the room, and two five-foot walkways on either side of a twenty-foot wide living space. There were also two twenty-foot wide living areas on the outside of each five-foot walkway, for a total of four distinct areas. However, these two areas were divided into ten-feet wide, by the usual twenty-feet long slots. Many of those two areas were further subdivided in half for the smallest of these larger animals and birds. It all had the appearance of a Red-Cross evacuation shelter. [ed. note: See what I mean? Even that organization has been around since before the beginning of time. That's the way it is with those who dedicate themselves to giving to others. Good works and selfless sacrifices are everlasting.]

After I communicated briefly and reassuringly with Olive, Graham, Elliott and Lois, I reminded them, given the significant number of the world's largest carnivores living in their area, that there was to be no nibbling on one another's neighbors. And in a more official capacity, I asked them to pass along to the other Voyage Committee members our need to meet in two days in the Wheel House at 10 a.m. I wanted to give everyone the next day to recover a bit of their composure and sense of well being.

I knew I was at the edge. Once I finished my survey of Nora and Noah's quarters, I was heading straight to bed. Emotionally, I was spent. Even if this excuse-for-a-boat sunk in the next few hours, I doubted at that moment it would have caused me much concern. All the preparations, worry, chaos and noise had finally taken up residence in my soul. And I was too weary to go on much further.

So, I did a cursory survey of Noah's family's living area. It was divided into five separate units. Three of them were for his three son's families and a smaller one for Nora and Noah. Throughout the entire voyage, it was only Nora and Noah who invited Holly and I into their living area. But the fifth area I was able to enter repeatedly. It was at the front entrance to their bow compartment. It was in here that they maintained three small bee hives. It also housed their own supplies, which consisted of farming and household implements, extra bedding and clothing, crockery and crates of food supplies and ceramic jars of all sizes, containing flour, wine, honey, sugar, beans, rice and water.

Most of all there were containers of water. It was the highest on Noah's list of worries. The risk of our running out of water was real and potentially life-ending for us all. And to prevent that from happening, we had lashed to the boat's top deck railing countless huge, empty, ceramic jars, in hopes of their being at least partially filled with water during the flooding period. But we had no idea if that would work.

The last of my inspections began with my poking at a large object with my staff; it was their indoor cooking box. It was positioned at the front entrance to the interior ramps, in hopes its smoke would rise, unimpeded, out the top deck's ramp entrance.

The cooking fire, which at that point was not lit, was held within a large wooden crate. I had watched it being built one day. On the bottom of the box one foot of sand was spread out evenly. Then on top of that was placed an additional twelve inches of porous, partially ground-up, volcanic rock. Next, slate-rock slabs were laid down on the top of the volcanic base, and parallel to all four sides, but kept two feet from the wooden box's outside walls. And again sand and volcanic rock was evenly poured around each side until it was even with the top of the box. On top was placed another, thinner slate-slab, which extending out over the volcanic rock sides, from one side to the other, leaving an opening into the fire pit on the other side of that top slab. The top slate had holes hollowed out in its face to allow heat to penetrate easily to the ceramic bowls that were placed on it. In those bowls, as Nora informed me a few days ago, would be water boiled for tea, soup or any other need that might arise during our trip.

And for later use, there was one other of these fire pits constructed to use on the top deck, once the rains stopped and the weather permitted its use.

Seeing that Noah's quarters appeared to be relatively calm, I decided it was time to make my way back to Holly and begin some needed rest. For me, this first day on Noah's ark was over. And most importantly by then, it had stopped rocking. The last thing I remembered was Holly lying down beside me and hearing the serenade from the chorus of eventide songbirds.

THIRTEEN: SETTLING IN

Aside from getting up at 7:45 a.m. the day after the flooding started, and just making it to Noah's first Watch Report from Ham, and my beginning to inscribe these reports on the walls of the Wheel House each morning, I didn't awaken fully until two days after we all boarded Noah's ark. And again, it was around 7:45 a.m. when I awoke. On that day I would also be hosting the second onboard Voyage Committee meeting, after I took the report of the three watches the day before.

Of course, by now you are wondering, among other things, how did anyone survive this Flood and the boat ride that followed? How could I rationalize that someone would be persistent and lucky enough to find this record buried deep within these limestone burrows and caves? Or how did I know what time of day it actually was all those years ago? You must be thinking, "Surely, we didn't have clocks or watches!" And you're right; we didn't. We just knew what time it was. It was innate in each of us who walked around or flew about the planet in those days. It was like talking, we just knew how to tell it. And come on, if there was a Flooding Event that covered the entire planet and if Noah was over 600 years old, as I rewrite this account on various tablets, what's not to believe about us being able to tell time. So don't get in a stitch about it. We just could.

Anyway, I reached over and gave Holly a peck on her cheek and whispered that I'd try to be back here for our late afternoon meal together. She mumbled something reassuring and snuggled down under our one blanket and continued her soft, murmuring sounds of deep sleep.

Once I made my way over to the ramps, I found that Carl had already come up from the fourth deck and that he, Paula and Glenda were all waiting for me. Together, we climbed into the ever-flowing river of occupants heading to and from the top deck Facilities, but first we had to pick up Olive and Graham on the second deck. And they, too, were waiting for us. It was so comforting to me to have these five dedicated companions to help guide and eventually to help keep order and peace on board this tossing menagerie of life forms.

Each one had their own unique characteristics, which together gave me great confidence that we might just complete this trip without a major incident. Glenda, with her huge, intensely staring eyes, was deliberate and thoughtful in all matters. What little humor she did have was dry and droll. And when she spoke, everyone listened intently. I often sought her out for advice and counsel. If there were others like her who came from Australia, I would gladly have made them my choice for trusted friends, if I had had the time to do so.

Carl, on the other hand, was more the Hollywood type [ed. note: Possibly you thought Merrill might describe him differently, but Show Business has been a part of daily life since my ancestors had the ability to speak. I found references everywhere in Merrill's notes of, "Oh, you're so 'Hollywood'!, I guess implying that they were showing off...or wanting a lot in payment for whatever little they just did...]. He was a night owl, so to speak. It was nothing to hear him calling "cuc...koo, cuc...koo" way into the night. And in a way, it was a reassuring call. But all the while he was singing, he was thinking. He was, by far, the intellectual of the group. Nighttime was when he did his best thinking. I would never know what scheme or idea he would come up with by the next morning. But almost every other day he'd meet me at the Wheel House and give me a synopsis of an issue or problem that he had puzzled over most of the previous night. And then, he'd offer his remedy to resolve it!

Olive, bless her heart, was a natural leader. Everyone, even Noah and his family, recognized her leadership qualities. She was thoughtful, not quick to judge, and sought reasonable compromise when opposing points of view had merit. But she also had a side of her that demanded you pay attention. She well understood that everyone's survival depended on avoiding foolish behavior and impulsive decisions. I trusted her completely.

Paula was the comedian. Hands down,

when the situation was becoming unbearable, she could come up with a one-liner that made all of us laugh. But behind her humor, there was savvy. She used her humor both to disarm and to relax those around her, but it also paved the way to address the crux of any issue that followed. In fact, you always knew that when her humor was at its best, there was a substantial comment about to be made and that you needed to get ready for it. She always brought any discussion into clear focus for a final decision.

And finally, there was Graham. Honestly, he was my favorite. If I had to be on a lifeboat, stranded in the middle of this Flooding Mess beyond the security of this boat, I'd want Holly, Lewis, Lois, Elliot, Elaine, Lance, Lolly, Stan and Graham right beside me. Granted, it would have to be a rather large lifeboat. But he'd somehow arrange to get one. His wisdom and ability to arbitrate were the stuff of fables. And, ultimately, he became the court judge for the entire boat. His thoughtfulness and fairness never ceased to amaze me. And as ferocious as he could look at times, he was as gentle a giant as there ever was. He became my best buddy, after Holly, of course.

After we all greeted each other in as pleasant a manner as circumstances would allow, both inside our over-crowded boat and outside it where the horrific-sounding storm was raging, I glanced over toward Noah's families' compartments and saw that Nora was tending a fire in their stand-alone fire pit.

I called out, "Top of whatever-kind-of-morning-this-is-about-to-be, Nora."

And she replied, "And the rest of it, which I

pray it-will-continue-to-provide-us-safe-passage, to you, Merrill."

"What are you cooking, so early this morning?"

"Merrill, I'm just boiling water," she answered. "To do anything else these days risks this fire getting out of control or me spilling or dumping everything on the floor if we should happen to hit a stretch of bad weather."

"You've got to be kidding!" I blurted out, needing to hurry on up to the Watch House for report, but stunned at her comment. "If the present circumstances don't represent 'a stretch of bad weather', then I want to be the first to request a transfer to another realm immediately. What could be worse than what's going on outside as we speak?"

"You never know, Merrill," she replied as calmly as if we were waking up to a sunny, spring day. "True, we haven't seen anything like this before, but who knows? It may get worse. So, I'm just going to try to boil water for my first cuppa tea since leaving home. Would you and your associates like some?"

"Something hot, or even warm, sounds heavenly," I couldn't help but say, and looking around at everyone else, they were nodding their heads in vigorous agreement. "But I have to get up topside for report. The other Committee members might be able to help you and have a drink themselves."

Suggesting that, I could see that all five were relieved and excited to help Nora in any way they could. It was a little gesture on her part, but it obviously meant so much to them.

And I thought to myself later that morning that if everyone could just sit down with one another once or twice a week over a cup of hot, steaming, Earl Grey tea, most of the world's woes would either be solved or at least soothed-out enough to be minimized. Coffee has a bitterness that leaves you a little too edgy for compromise and making lasting resolutions. Rum is too good to drink in moderation and you eventually will lose any meaningful focus. Hot tea is the drink of choice for a world wanting to achieve any semblance of cooperation and well being. It civilizes and calms our innate meanness.

And before I could turn and encourage them to cross over to Nora's fire pit, they were half way there anyway. She was adored by each of them from that moment on. And it was a relationship that lasted for years to follow, to the betterment of all.

For me, I requested they be at the Wheel House by 9 a.m., and then I began my walk up the final ramp into the Ramp House.

As I walked, I wondered just how Nora was able to boil water in that ceramic bowl. Then I remembered that one day I did ask Noah about that kind of activity, when I saw him having some hot soup for lunch. He told me then that water could be boiled in ceramic bowls now because they were given a second firing with a glaze coating spread over them before that final firing in their rather crude-appearing kiln.

I next asked what glaze was. It sounded to

me like something you smear on a cupcake or rum cake.   ...You can see right away that I appear partial to that wonderful spirit... and who wouldn't be? Besides, it became the drink of choice aboard ships at sea, which we were... unfortunately given our present circumstances... the first... And Noah explained to me that glaze is a form of glass that is modified to melt and bond to clay, and that it consists of three substances: silica, alumina and flux. How he'd come up with all these discoveries, I'd never guess, but given that he was over 600 years old as of this writing, I decided he had plenty of time to tinker with odd sorts of things like 'glazes'.

Further, he instructed me that day that silica or glass is commonly called sand, quartz or flint and that granite, found most everywhere on the planet's surface is the most commonly used source of silica. But he found that these glass compounds alone cannot be used for a glaze coating of his and Nora's clay pots. That was because the melting point for glass is 3100° F. That is far above the melting point of their clay pottery. And if they tried a second firing in the kiln with just glass, it would melt their pots.

So he found that you had to add a flux, which lowered glasses' melting point to an acceptable level. He used borax, which he found in abundance just a few miles west of his farm and that did the trick. And finally, he had to add alumina or feldspar to the glaze mixture to allow its coating to shrink or bond onto the pottery being fired a second time. And by the end of that second firing, he then had a container that not only held water but that was able to withstand boiling water inside it, which at 212° F. is far below the firing temperatures of pottery and glaze. And behold, all these elements combined provided the eager Voyage Committee their first cup of hot tea.

As I rose onto the top deck, the awful sounds of nearing out-of-control wind, rain and thunder again greeted me. The storm was undiminished in intensity; it was obvious. And you could hardly see anything beyond the railings of the boat. I thought in the few glances I cast, as I ran over to the Wheel House, that I still saw the hillsides that surrounded Noah's farm, but that there was no sign of trees or structures anywhere. The water level appeared to have risen far above them, and the hilltop where Holly's and my burrow used to be did not appear to be much higher. Like a bathtub being filled with water, Nora and Noah's valley appeared about to overflow. And up until now, we had simply been bouncing around in circles within it. Relentlessly, it continued to fill at the same, unimaginable rate of nearly 15 feet per hour.

Using that as the benchmark for the entire forty day and night period, with Noah's property being at 440 foot elevation and our burrow sitting atop a 1500 foot outcrop of hills surrounding his farm, it was going to take close to three days for the rising water to top his valley's natural barricade. I expected the next day to prove very interesting if my calculations were correct.

For now, I needed to hurry over to the

Wheel House and get yesterday's reports from Japheth. On the way over, I was reminded of the argument that he'd put forth that a six-inch, slatted and elevated walkway needed to be installed from the Ramp House to the Restroom Facilities. Further, he felt it imperative to have a six-inch elevated sill around the entire top deck ramp opening, even though it was to be covered with a roof. His suggestion was met with considerable resistance; everyone by that time was exhausted from the structural challenges of just building this blasted boat. But somehow he prevailed. And later everyone was so thankful that he did. Throughout The Flood, it was to prevent our tracking wet footprints into the boat. Amazingly, the inside ramps were always as dry as the day they were installed. Japheth was a very practical-minded fellow, and I trusted his judgment as well.

Once inside the Wheel House, I got his report, which was basically the same as the one the day before. It highlighted that the ark's interior remained leak-free and that we were still confined inside Noah's valley, hemmed in by its surrounding high hills. Everyone was nervous about what would happen when we topped the hills and actually began to move beyond it. We knew we'd lose forever the relative serenity of that place and were petrified at what might lay ahead. In addition, we had no way to steer or propel this bloated barge anywhere. We would be completely at the mercy of existing currents, the wind and, I hoped, Noah's **Floodmaster**. Even then, there was considerable discussion beginning as to where we were eventually going to make landfall. Would we just bob up and down and then come back onto Noah's place? Or would we be shuttled to the outer reaches of our continental landmass, where all the earth quaking was taking place? No one knew. So we just worried and dreaded.

After writing the previous day's report on the Wheel House wall, all the Committee members showed up at 9 a.m., including Nora and Shem. Noah, as always during those first few weeks, was there for the beginning of the day's first watch. Olive, the Committee Chair, soon called the meeting to order and the discussion began with our previously outlined agenda, made weeks ago.

Fortunately, to make matters simple for us that day, Noah had already organized the Watch List and Log. His doing that freed us up to pursue the next agenda item, which was to develop a process for handling grievances and complaints.

It was eventually decided, as mentioned earlier in this record, that Graham would be the judge to arbitrate these issues amongst all the animals and birds on board. He would hold court, if you will, once a week in the cafeteria area, starting at 10 a.m. and lasting, if necessary until the late afternoon meal began. There could be no notices posted for each meeting.

*Only Holly and I could write them, and no one else knew how to read! What a fine mess that was. At the very least the **Floodmaster** could have waited until we all had at least that ability. Probably that's part of the reason we all got into this Flood Mess to begin with. Not enough people,* *animals and birds could write or read. Talk is really cheap. It's not until you see what you just said in print that you realize just how stupid it was. My feeling is that if and when everyone has that ability that they will then have to write down what they had just said and repeat it aloud again. Maybe after doing that, it will become more obvious to them what turkeys (my apologies for any unintended slur here...) they sometimes sound like. Anyway, we were all relieved that Graham agreed to accept this challenge. He was, as I said earlier, one of Holly's and my favorite folks on this trip and forever thereafter.*

A subcommittee was then formed to explore if any entertainment, lectures, skits or talent shows could be organized to help pass the time. We would have to hold any such boat-wide gatherings on the second deck; it being the only one that was not subdivided either by Noah's family or by the stored supplies and cafeteria. And it was decided they could plan on having something once a month, if there were enough participants and interest. For me, just having those magnificent birds sing, as they still did each evening, would be enough for me. But they thought there probably was other talent on board as well. They enlisted Holly to be on that subcommittee, mainly because of her ability to write, in case anyone wanted to develop a skit or a play of some kind.

Next, there was some discussion about guiding or steering the boat or at least determining the direction and speed we were traveling. No one, and I mean no one, was comfortable with what appeared at that time to be our bob-along propulsion system or with a Let's-Just-Wait-and-See-Where-We-End-Up navigational approach. Drifting wasn't going to cut it. And we were all scared witless what was going to happen when we topped the hills the next day. Would there be a torrent of raging water that swept us into some mammoth whirlpool or into a steep, narrow canyon that boxed us in and submerged us all? Or would we be swept out into a vast ocean, never to see any land again? None of us were comfortable just perched in the Wheel House, with its ridiculous steering wheel, connected to absolutely nothing but its upright floor stand. Maybe it fooled Noah into thinking he was charging into unexplored regions, "Where no woman, man, animal or bird has gone before," [ed. note: And, yes, even earlier expressions that we repeat so casually now were often used in those prehistoric times.] but we all knew better. We sensed we were simply going to drift into endless darkness, which may eventually contain some land. But unless we got a handle on our direction and speed, coupled with some method to determine when and if we were over flooded land or in Open Ocean, the rest of us knew we were in a hopeless situation.

My vote was to explore how to navigate away from all liquid, of any size or description. As I've already mentioned, being in or near water is not my comfort zone. I'm a desert and sand kind of fellow. Maybe a sprinkle of moisture once or twice a year is plenty for me. Oceans of water surrounding me represents a total failure on my part to communicate both my deepest needs and desires. If found in that circumstance, I would have no other choice than to... quit and leave.

The next to the last agenda item, which we had previously been charged with, was to organize a subcommittee to address the issues surrounding when and how to exit this ship of "What's Left", as I so often began to call it. Everyone thought it was too soon to get real serious about this subject, but this was one subcommittee I wanted to be on. Mainly because I wanted to be the first to get off. *One of my goals during this trip was to learn how to fly.*

And finally, as an issue raised by Olive in the "Are There Any Other Items to Discuss" portion of our meeting, she said there were some growing complaints that the birds and animals that were roosting, grooming or napping above the deck level were causing some mumbling from the deck occupants. It seems that there was a growing amount of midges, mites, feathers and hair filtering down onto the citizens resting below. And it probably had to be addressed soon. As a temporary solution, after considerable discussion and some rather heated exchanges between Paula, Glenda and Carl, all of whom have perches or roosts above Olive and Graham, who were obviously deck-bound, it was agreed that each region needed to be notified by members on this Committee that if you need to groom or nit-pick, go up to the top deck and do it. And to be fair, that included those who were deck-bound as well.

It ultimately made for some real congestion around the Ramp House, until the rain stopped. So much of that activity was stress-related. Before this voyage, it was just something most of us do to pass time. *I find myself picking midges from time to time, as well. And there's nothing in this world as satisfying as a good scratch... nothing. So this last Committee meeting issue involved all of us.*

With that discussion, our second Committee Meeting ended, and we left Nora, who was on second watch, for that third day of rainfall. Noah was going to stay with her for a while after we left to acquaint her with how she would probably manage the following watch. The rest of us ran back to the Ramp House or Restrooms. We knew tomorrow would reveal some major changes in our lives. And I desperately wanted to go back to sleep until then.

But once I was able to work my way through the surging throngs of life moving along the walkways, ramps and deck aisles to Holly, I found her visiting with all our old friends, Lewis, Lois, Elliot, Elaine, Lance, Lolly, Stan and Fran. It was the beginning of an agreed upon arrangement where we would all meet in the cafeteria area each morning at around 10:30 a.m. to simply chat. [ed. note: Consider this the first, recorded reference to a "coffee clutch" in all prehistory; minus the coffee, of course. But, honestly, I'm not sure how you'd 'clutch', in any meaningfully way, onto an elephant.] The only day of the week we didn't meet was when Graham was using the area for his chambers. But even on that day when an upcoming issue was one that fascinated us, we would come anyway and just listen to him make his decisions and occasionally pronounce an accompanying sentence. And as time passed, it was this same group that would plan and orchestrate our departure, once this bob-along-boat was finally able to discharge its passengers and cargo. I honestly think it was the relationship that Holly had with Lois and Elaine that kept her sane during all that confinement.

I know Lewis and Elliot kept my bubble centered on most days. But there were days when I freely admit my bubble was anything but level. And the morning of that fourth day, since the rain began and after our third, full day encased in this ever-circling circus, was my most tilted one.

I arose that same morning, gave Holly a hug, grabbed my staff and staggered up the gangways to the Ramp House. By now the raging noise from the storm, although unchanged, had almost taken on the quality of 'white noise'. You nearly didn't hear it! And when all the racket stopped after forty straight days and nights of it, the resulting silence was absolutely deafening. Believe me. And that silence was also almost more frightening. You were waiting in expectation for the next big event: the world to open up and swallow you, a tidal wave to wash you leagues under the sea or a comet to land in your lap. Whatever catastrophe it was to be, you knew for sure it wasn't going to be a minor one. Our disaster appetites had been whetted. We now expected the very worst to occur, something totally beyond all belief. No house fire would do. We needed something equal to the worldly collapse then taking place around us to be impressed or moved. We were becoming a jaded bunch of survivors. But not just yet.

Because what I saw that morning coming out on the top deck was as disturbing as anything before or since. It was not a mind-flash of the end of the world; we were already in the grips of that kind of disaster. It was seeing the final remnants of life clinging onto the last vestige of hillside where Holly's and my burrow used to be. [See the accompanying Appendix: "THE DELUGE".]

As I looked eastward that morning, through the torrents of rain, I simply stopped dead, and stared at the last 100 feet of earth not yet submerged in the unrelenting rainfall. And on that patch of sandy soil were literally hundreds, if not thousands, of animals of all sizes, along with a few dozen people, some of whom I recognized as being the ones who tried to scalp me that day Lewis rescued me. And they all were screaming at us as we passed by them. They were all drowning, one by one, before my eyes. Oddly, I remember there were no birds. The last of them didn't appear until later. And as we were lifted up by the ever-rising flood waters, our boat simply slipped by them, like a ghost. I had no feeling of triumph or privilege; and when I eventually forced myself to go on to the Wheel House, neither did Noah, the only occupant inside it.

Noah spoke first after I closed the door. "I have no idea what is ahead for us, and I feel no pride or relief at being left on board this vessel right now. Merrill, seeing what you have just observed is as devastating to me as I'm sure it is to you.

Luckily, it is only you and I that will have witnessed this heart-wrenching sight. My having the last watch last night and you having the first watch this morning, is a kind of blessing. If others on board saw what we've just have, I fear it would have sunk this ark, as sure as if we'd struck an outcrop of rocks and breached the hull. I must ask that you never share with Holly or anyone else what we've just seen. Even before mentioning it in your future record of this effort of ours should probably be kept secret. Only those who eventually ever read your account of our time together will see the retelling of what we've just seen. It says too much. And I'm so sorry you saw it."

I was unable to speak for a while, but eventually I was able to reply, as I guess any soldier must when faced with a duty that has been assigned to him or her, "Yes, chief, I'd give almost anything to not have seen it, but I will promise to respect your request. No good will come from describing it to anyone on board this ark of yours. Maybe it might warn others in the times to come, but it has no value for us in this place and time."

And no more was ever discussed between us about what we both saw that morning.

FOURTEEN: THE ENDLESS SEA

My first day's watch was painfully slow, given what Noah and I had just witnessed and there being no one around to at least share some companionship. But, in a way, I was glad Holly did not come up. She did have the next watch, so it was appropriate she rested until then. Besides, I would have been too tempted to describe to her what I saw and what I would have heard, if it hadn't been for the roaring of The Storm.

But, Noah, bless his heart, did send Lewis and Elliot up to visit with me. Somehow, he knew that with my closet guy friends, we'd probably talk about nothing of any real significance, other than about the priceless matters that any lasting friendship spawns. With their arrival, the rest of my watch passed quickly and with much less pain.

You may wonder how Elliot was able to enter the Wheel House. As was mentioned somewhere before, the Wheel House was twenty-five feet to a side. The stern-facing door was eight feet wide, just enough to comfortably accommodate the likes of Elliot and Elaine. And on the bow end of the room was our single, recessed window, with its sheltering, external overhang. About three feet behind it was the Ship's Wheel, mounted on its sturdy pedestal. The center of the room had a ten-foot long table, with enough room at the starboard side for Elliot or Elaine to stand, sit or lie, depending on whether they were on watch duty, attending a meeting or just visiting with someone like me. There were wooden chairs on two sides and a long bench on another. Two other benches were against the port and starboard walls. The room was paneled in knotty pine, giving it a warm, welcoming atmosphere. It was, come to think of it, one of the most consistently occupied areas on board the ship, other than the Restroom Facilities, that is. They seemed to be a magnet. I never realized...

The conversation that day between the three of us was light banter. It was as if we were making a subconscious effort to deny The Storm's presence in our lives. And by 3:45 p.m. Holly joined us. I gave her my report, minus the horror Noah and I had seen earlier. But I did describe that devastating scene on the Wheel House's wall log. Interestingly, for some reason Holly never read what I wrote up there. I figured she thought it was probably just boring, boat-related jabber. When, in fact, it was filled with emotionally laden impressions and incidents. It was a kind of therapy for me, and it provided the background for what you are now reading.

My report being finished and Holly appearing comfortable with taking The Watch, I hurried back to our berth, laid down for an hour and then went to the cafeteria for my only meal that day. I was famished. It was a serving of dried fruit, some seeds, a couple sprigs of alfalfa, and a small piece of jerky. Tasty, huh. Mostly, though, I was thirsty. That, I knew, was going to be the Achilles' heel for this voyage: quenching everyone's thirst. [ed. note: I know, I know, Achilles wasn't suppose to exist for another two or three jillion years. But how do you think Achilles' parents came up with that name in the first place?... Now you're catching on.]

FIFTEEN: THE STRETCH

The rain and deafening noise continued for the next thirty-six days and nights, non-stop. There was no way to really know how much rain had fallen, but you had to guess it was enough. I wasn't sure what determined when it should stop, but I also wasn't involved in any way in the decision to start it. But, thankfully, it did end. However, that's another, WHOLE other story in itself. The stopping was almost more terrifying than The Storm itself.

It was, again, on the morning of my second Watch that this paralyzing event occurred. I had been delayed, somewhat, by having to settle an argument between some of the larger animals on the second deck. It required that I listen to each one and then make a snap judgment. *Actually, there is hardly any other kind I ever make. I leave it to Holly and Graham to be pensive, deliberate and decisive. I'm the impulsive one, and somehow they seem to respect or at least tolerate that about me.*

Anyway, I came up onto the top deck at 7:59 a.m., amidst the usual thundering, blowing racket of the now-I-was-convinced-this-was-going-to-be-a-

174

forever-rainstorm, and at 8 a.m. sharp, exactly forty days after it began… it stopped!! The clouds disappeared just as suddenly, and the sun shown as bright as any desert sun I'd ever experienced. Looking up at the wonderfully clear, blue sky was overwhelming, and I was just about to let out a huge yell in celebration, when I looked down and saw it for the first time. It was the most awesome, overwhelming, petrifying moment of my entire life. I was staring for the first time at the ocean!

It stretched forever, in every direction. There were no trees, no outcrops of hills or mountains, which I'd only heard about. And there was definitely no level land. All I saw was a world of water, framed only by the horizon. I turned in circles over and over, hoping to see something that might be a landmark. All I could see were the undulating, endless swells of a nameless, featureless and absolutely bewildering body of water. I knew immediately we were and always would be hopelessly lost in this forever. There was no way to determine where you were or where you were going, or how fast you got to one or were getting to the other.

Standing there, the only thing I could think to do was suggest to Noah that as soon as I got into the Wheel House for our change of Watch, I immediately go get Glenda and Carl; and we begin to think what to do to about somehow charting our course or at least determine the direction and how fast we were getting somewhere.

Once inside the Wheel House, I found Noah standing at the window, mute and dumbfounded.

He, too, was staggered by what lay ahead and all around us. There were no topographical landmarks or features to orient us. We felt we were the first earthly beings to see Open Ocean, much less to be wandering aimlessly about on it. Not even shorebirds at that time ventured into this realm. They didn't have to. Pangaea was all one land mass. Anyone venturing out into this wilderness was doomed to get lost. With my suggestion, he readily agreed I go below and get them.

Without another word to him, I laid my staff on the bench, where I sat most of the time I was on Watch or at a meeting of some kind, and rushed back across the top deck and down into the third deck to find Glenda. Luckily, Carl had joined her there, which meant I didn't have to then go to the fourth one for him. They were engaged in an intense discussion about something they called "pi, a mathematical constant." [ed. note: See What I Mean!!] I hated to interrupt them, but whatever they were arguing about was certainly not as urgent as what Noah and I had just seen.

"You, guys, hold on!" I called out breathlessly. And then I paused briefly to catch enough of it to explain why I was there. "Noah and I need you immediately in the Watch House!" I finally exclaimed.

"Why?" Glenda asked, not yet having noticed the silence outside the boat, due to all the background noise that normally existed inside this third deck from the infinite numbers of engaged and conversing life forms.

"Because The Storm has stopped and

something worse, if that could be imaged, has taken its place!" I stammered, now becoming even more nervous and panicky as I answered her question.

"And what could that be?" Carl followed up.

"You'll have to wait and see. I'm unable to tell or describe it to you adequately. You have to see for yourselves. HURRY! We need you. All of us on board this potentially doomed ship need you to follow me RIGHT NOW!!"

With that, I said no more and whipped my head to the side, indicating we had to head back up the ramps to the top deck. And once we exited the Ramp House's enclosure and they could see what lay before them, for as far as the eye, any eye, could see, they both gasped.

"What is all that?" Glenda asked her voice filled with absolute wonder.

"Beats me," I replied, "but as you see, it's all around us. It and NOTHING, I mean NOTHING, else! And that's why Noah and I needed you right away. As you can see, we are lost somewhere in the middle of all this water.

I later thought, once my brain had shifted from the terrified mode to simply the usual, overwhelmed one, that the ocean was most likely related to what Stan and his fellow, long-range travelers called "The Stretch", but I was sure even he had never seen anything quite like this. WE WERE IN THE MIDDLE OF IT!!

Once inside the Wheel House and seated around the table, Noah and I began to outline what, at a minimum, we needed to somehow know. Basically, it was where we were. Then where we were heading? And finally, how fast we were getting there? And because it was my Watch, I didn't expect Holly to relieve me for another seven and a half hours. Between now and then, I hoped these two could come up with some answers. I couldn't bear to face her without being able to give some reassurance that we knew, at least vaguely, in what direction we were heading.

Immediately after Noah's and my pleas, the two Voyage Committee members began a serious conference between themselves, in which occasionally one of them would raise their voice. In the meantime, Noah and I went over to the window and stared out at the vastness before us, completely bewildered as to what to do next.

After about thirty minutes, Glenda and Carl called out to us to follow them out onto the open deck where we could visualize the rising Sun. Feeling a slight sense of relief that they might be onto something, Noah and I hurried outside behind them.

Stopping at the starboard-side railing, Glenda asked that we briefly note the position of the Sun, and then follow her hand as she traced its probable path across the sky that day to the other side of the boat. Following those directions, she next had us turn and she pointed toward the stern of the boat and traced her hand from that direction over us to the bow section.

After doing that she said, for the first time in pre-recorded history, "Carl and I have decided that we have to designate and name these four directions that I have just pointed out to you. They are to be designated the four 'Cardinal Directions'; and for their names we've taken the abbreviations for what has happened or is about to happen.

"In the order that I pointed them out, they are: "Every Animal Stayed There", meaning the Delta located in that same direction from your farm, Noah; and it is to be the 'EAST'. The opposite direction to it is: "Where Even Stan Traveled", meaning that Stan, the Messenger stork, occasionally traveled in that direction; and it is to be the 'WEST'. For the direction to the aft of us, it is: "Some of Us Tried Here", meaning it was an area not frequently on anyone's itinerary; and it is to be 'SOUTH'. And finally the last direction, corresponding to where our bloated barge is presently heading it is: "Noah Often Regrets This Heading; and it is to be 'NORTH'". [ed. note: I rest my case.]

I excitedly exclaimed, "That's Great! Really Great!! But how do we know we're going in any particular direction at night or during daylight when the sun is hidden under clouds, even though I can't imagine there being any more clouds left anywhere after what we've just been through."

"That's our next project," Carl answered. "But you're going to have to give us a little more time to tackle that problem."

And for you, the hoped-for and eventual reader of this entire log, in my retelling what happened during our voyage, its aftermath and what preceded it at Noah's farm; I freely incorporated these four cardinal designations that Carl and Glenda gave us that day.

There then followed another period of intense discussion between Glenda and Carl, which at one point entailed their reaching over and examining my shepherd's staff. Once they examined it, they inquired how and where I got it. The only answer I could give was that Holly made it before I traveled through the Delta region, and that they would have to ask her for more details when she came on duty at 4 p.m. today for her Watch. I then asked why they cared to know.

Pointing to the straight end of the staff, Carl asked Noah and me to take a close look at it, something I had never done. I just always grabbed it and went off about my business. But at their request, I was surprised to see countless specks of material clinging to the end of it, and that underneath them was a very hard, rock-like material. Holly had embedded it into the wooden shaft. It was intended to keep me from wearing the bottom of the staff off when I walked along or banged it.

Glenda then said, "That is just like the material I was tinkering with back home, in an area with hillsides littered with hardened, reddish rocks. I found that some of them actually attracted other bits of gravel and that they would cling to these other, odd-acting rocks. Over time, I examined their properties further and found if I rubbed one of these rock-clinging stones over others similar to it, they too then had that same ability. I called this activity 'magnetizing'. And what was even more curious, was when I did that to thinner slivers of those same stones and placed them on some kind of pivot to balance them, they always pointed in the same direction.

"Carl and I have noticed that Holly also inlaid some of those same stones, as are at the base, around the bottom sides of your staff for decoration. If it is ok with you, Merrill, we'd like to pry one of those slivers out and see if we can rub it with the end of your staff and see what happens."

"Sure," I replied, by now completely dumbfounded as to how all this was going to play out.

And to my amazement, over the next ten minutes, these two Voyage Committee members, now become prehistoric scientists and inventors, worked feverishly at that task. And at one point Carl turned to me and asked if I would go down to the cafeteria and ask Nora or whoever was on duty there if I could have a small ceramic bowl, half filled with the oil that we use for our taper lamps. And then I was to bring both of these back up here as soon as possible.

After about thirty minutes of scurrying around to get what he requested, I hurried back and found that Noah and the two inventors were looking down at a thin, two inch long, pointed flake of material, taken from my staff. Quickly, as soon as I set the partially filled bowl on the table, they gently placed the shaving on top of the oil. Surprisingly, it was light enough, and the oil thick enough, that it floated on its surface; and most amazing of all, it jiggled, twisted a bit and then stopped moving pointing in a specific direction. When it did, Glenda asked me to mark a line with my chalk on the top lip of the bowl at both ends the sliver was pointing toward. They then asked that Noah gently pick up the bowl and take it outside the Wheel House and place it on the deck.

Once we all went outside and Noah set the bowl down, we watched the same behavior of the small, floating pointer happen again. And again, it pointed in that same, exact direction as before, lining up with my chalk marks. At that point, Glenda asked that we notice where the Sun was rising from and trace its approximate path across the sky to where it would set that evening. After we did that, she observed and exclaimed, "The arrow is pointing exactly between the East and West directions. It's showing us North and South!!" It was the first, ever, "Eureka Moment".

We never gave their bowl a name, but it was kept safely tucked inside a special box that Noah had Ham build for it. And I'm sure by the time you read this, it must have a name. We just called it our "Pointer Bowl". [ed. note: Yep, it was the first compass, which up until now was credited to the Chinese or some Mesoamericans over 3000 years ago. This was as big a surprise to me as I'm sure it is to you.]

This discovery was followed by some rather hectic activity in which Noah, Ham and Shem were asked to remove the lowest cross-board on the railing between two of the restroom facilities at the middle portion of the stern, top deck. Once they had removed it, they were then instructed by Carl to shape a curved, triangle-shape board about twelve inches across at its curved bottom and ten inches long at its two triangle-shaped sides. Then they were to drill out holes at the three corners of the triangle [ed. note: Think kite.] and secure rope through each hole, tying it off about two feet away from the board, and attach another 150 foot long rope to that loop.

The longer rope was then secured to a reel that was mounted between the railing posts that had been holding the plank Noah and Ham removed earlier. And, again, it was centered exactly at the middle of the stern section.

At the bottom of the curved wooden triangle, another hole was to be drilled at its center and attached to it was another strand of rope, tied to a leather pouch with a ten pound rock inside. The rock was to be taken from the ones that we had used to weigh down the sides of the wood-covered tent walkway. It would serve to weigh the wooden board down enough that it wouldn't float, but sink enough to provide the needed resistance to our boat's forward movement.

Then we had to throw this contraption overboard at the stern and estimate what the distance was along the rope when the wooden wedge actually hit the water and began resisting the ship's movement. *Remember that the top deck is 30-40 feet above the waterline.* At that point, we were to tie a large knot of colored ribbon along the rope's length, and then measure out 48 feet two times and tie the same bundle of ribbon at each of those distances. In addition, we tied smaller knots of ribbon every 4.8 feet to give us tenths of that same 48 foot distance. *Glenda was a stickler for detail*... And supposedly, this would to tell us how fast we were going when that first ribbon left the top deck and I counted: "1, one thousand; 2, one thousand; 3, one thousand; 4, one thousand; 5, one thousand" six times or for 30 seconds. At that moment we were to note how many larger and smaller ribbons had gone overboard.

When I asked her why 48 feet specifically, she replied that it was because it was equal to 6 fathoms. I then asked her what a "fathom" was, and she just shrugged and said it's something like a "cubit".

Right then, I realized how little I had in common with the scientific mind. And to add to my self-awareness of this intellectual void, I asked her what final information we got after this tying off, heaving, uncoiling and counting. She replied, in equally obtuse terms, the "nautical miles per hour" that Noah's ark was traveling.

And so we began, as of 11 a.m. that same morning, taking readings every day at that same hour, me counting off the 30 "one thousands", and Ham or Shem throwing the wooden slab overboard, with Glenda or Carl doing the observing and noting the number of ribbons that left the reel in that timeframe.

Oddly enough, and to their every lasting credit, that first day the number that came up was 0.9 nautical miles per hour. And it was consistently that number the next 150 days. Carl and Glenda calculated that it had to have been that same speed for the prior 36 days during The Flood, after we stopped spinning in circles in Nora and Noah's valley those first four days of rainfall. And when they added all the miles up for our entire trip, we had traveled precisely 4,000 nautical miles to our final destination. The speed we measured each day didn't vary, even when we performed additional ones throughout any given day. We ended up calling our speed the "Glenda/Carl Constant", figuring it had to be the speed any ark might travel, if another one, heaven forbid, was built for another one of these Flood events.

By noon that day Glenda and Carl had somehow managed to achieve major scientific breakthroughs that I'm sure have gone completely unsung for most of time. We were so proud of them. All that was left now was establishing some sense of the shape of this planet. We had the migrating birds telling us that we were now sailing on a curved surface. With that information as a starting point, Carl reminded us, as we sat around that Wheel House table, that whenever the Moon was in its full phase, it looked like a ball. And, as well, he informed us that any material that is, or has evolved into a sphere, is then at its most stable and enduring shape. Therefore, he and Glenda surmised that our world, wet to the gills that it was at that moment, was round as well.

And that being the case, they decided there had to be a middle point, one that dissected the planet in half, an "equator", they called it. And to prove that, they further surmised that if we looked at the stars visible at night, that at some point they will stop drifting northward and would simply trace directly overhead throughout that night. When that was observed, we will be at our planet's equator. From there, we would then be heading into the northern "latitudes"; another of those words that the two of them threw around so casually. *It was all so complicated to me.*

But what was decided was that each night, the person starting the first Watch would note the drifting of a particular cluster of stars, or "constellations", as they called them, to see if they drifted either north or south or moved straight over our boat.

The next thing we all did, as kind of as a classroom exercise, was to take the techniques and discoveries made that day and employ them at our present location.

Given we had already traveled for thirty-six days, and assuming a constant speed of 0.9 knots per hour, which was our speed then, as now, we calculated we have sailed (or 'bobbed' would be the more accurate description) 777 nautical miles thus far to that point. And by what the jiggling sliver in the ceramic bowl continually indicated, we were on a heading of North by Northeast. [ed. note: See the accompanying Appendix: "THE ARK'S HEADING TO MT. ARARAT"] Glenda and Carl hadn't devised any numerical values yet for the Pointer Bowl's apparent circle that the sliver could trace. That would come later. Certainly, all in all, it was a very satisfying day's work.

I confirmed their entire day's findings and headings exactly one week later when I came to the Wheel House to write my routine log entries on the wall. Paula, who was just coming off first watch, reported to me that the Aquarius cluster or constellation, and more specifically Mars, the planet we named and watched cross the African sky, had not shifted northward all night. She kept going out to observe, and seeing no upward motion of any stars, she became suspicious that something strange was happening.

Excitedly, I shouted, "We were at the equator!"

And giving me almost as much satisfaction as their discovery, before she said anything further, I was able to come to that conclusion, without anyone coaching me.

To celebrate that fact, we had our first all-boat party that night. Everyone acted silly, and we danced to the musical instruments that Nora and Noah's family played. As a finale, we all sang songs, which when you combine the voices of a relatively few humans with that of thousands of animals and birds, it was quite a planetary chorus. The more we all sang, the louder it got. And Holly and I thought later, the more lovely it all became.

It was like we were both mourning, which we had not had the chance to do formally, and saluting those who were not there with us. It was as rich a sound as the earth smells when it is prepared for a harvest of grain or grass. It celebrated life, in all its manifestations, that was present on that giant life boat. And you couldn't help but wish somehow it could have been recorded to be played for all the generations that hopefully would follow us. There still was no laughter anywhere on that boat of survivors, nor was there any throughout the voyage.

*And I didn't expect any until the time Holly and I
moved on to maybe another life form, after we'd
finished our assignments in this one. But song
replaced it. Only you that follow will hopefully
have the goodness and blessing of laughing and
singing all in one day. That was not to be our fate
after The Storm began.*

But that was not the only surprise that I had
that same day after Paula's discovery.. After I had
finished my Watch Log entries, I left the Wheel
House to join Holly for a late breakfast. And as I
closed the Wheel House door, glancing straight
ahead toward the Ramp House, I noticed that there
were no other boat occupants on this portion of the
top deck yet. There was still a morning chill in the
air, but come afternoon, it would be jammed with
sun-bathers and those just seeking fresh sea air.

It was at that moment that I heard a call,
"Hey, is there anyone else around who could give
us a hand?"

Stunned, I turned and saw perched on the
port railing, a few feet away from the Wheel House,
a very large, never before seen, bird. "Who are
you?" I blurted out, nearly stumbling and falling
over my staff. "And where did you come from?
How did you get here?"

"My name is Archie, and my companion,
who should be arriving momentarily, is Alice. We
came from 'out there', and we are so relieved to
have found you. Do you know there is nowhere to
roost... anywhere? Everything, and I mean
everything, is covered with water! If it weren't for
our raft, we all would have drowned for certain.

And as for how we got anywhere near here, that should be somewhat obvious; we flew, in case you hadn't noticed we're birds, Albatrosses, to be more precise. I've understood that some folks like to call us 'gooney birds'. We'd prefer, if you don't mind, that moniker not be used any longer. As far as we're concerned, what's gooney, goofy and truly gruesome is This Flood! What's that all about? One day it starts raining, after we'd experienced months of thick, black, very loud clouds; and it doesn't stop for weeks. You couldn't even call it rain; that implies the presence of rain drops. This was like an onrushing river pounding down on your head. We nearly drowned simply by being perched on that raft! It was absolutely awful, believe me.

"Our survival has been due to each of us pitching in and catching fish and bolstering each other's spirits, when one of us got down. But then, out of the blue-green world we all seemed to exist in anymore, this huge, floating, tree-lined, box-shaped form appeared on the horizon. And it headed straight for us. We swore you were aiming at us."

"Who else is with you, besides Alice?" I inquired cautiously, concerned that there might be a thousand more mouths to feed.

"There are six more," Archie answered, the tone of his voice displaying a sense of pride in what they had accomplished, surviving on the world's first and only, totally flooded planet. "They consist of two emperor penguins, two pelicans and two frigate birds. You'll meet them all in a few moments, but you'll have to rig up a rescue basket to lift the penguins up onto this deck. There's no way they can hop up this 30 or 40 foot height. The other four will be flying up, as soon as I give them the 'thumbs up' that it's all ok. We were sure you wouldn't be all humans, which we figured had something to do with this mess getting started in the first place. Believe me, you're a welcome sight for rain and sea-soaked eyes."

What followed for the remainder of that day were Noah and his families pulling together the necessary rope lengths and a large enough basket to haul up the penguins.

And I probably should note that our baskets had also been used as a major source for storage and transport of food and other supplies. I realize I have overlooked that in my description of how we managed to load and store our supplies. And they were of all shapes and sizes, as well.

For lifting the penguins, Nora was able to empty the largest one, with a reinforced handle. In the days and weeks that followed, we used it to lower them back into the water, as well as for lifting them up onto the top deck, along with all the fish that our newcomers caught for us. Because our floating hotel only traveled less than one knot per hour, it wasn't like we had to launch and retrieve it off the stern. We simply used the port or starboard sides for this activity. And the rope lengths were spliced from the ropes that Elliot, Elaine and the others used to pull the ramp onto the top deck.

It was a blessing that those birds found us. The fish that they caught gave us the needed protein and vitamins to survive, and that I believe without a doubt. They were welcomed immediately into our community. And because they were found as we floated northward over what used to be Africa, they were assigned to that region's sleeping quarters. Their open-sea exploits made for great "Midnight Tall Tales", a time of camaraderie, semi-truths and comforting. Each region had this same activity and once a week we shared the best of the best in a boat-wide contest. It was one of the few lighter activities we engaged in during the entire voyage.

SIXTEEN: PASSING SCENERY, A MUTINY
AND ANOTHER STORM

By the evening of our 48th day since we passed over Holly's and my home site on that forlorn and tragic hilltop above Nora and Noah's farm, we saw our first and only landmass. Before and after that, all the way to our final destination, there were no topographical formations of any kind... only water. For all of us, to see what appeared on our eastern horizon that early evening was a great relief. We had all begun to think that water would be forever covering all the Earth, leaving none of us, aside from the sea creatures who dwelled in this all-encompassing ocean, a chance of survival.

Appropriate enough, it was just after our last meal for the day when Lance, Lolly, Stan and Fran, who were all perched on the starboard railing, first caught sight of it.   Lance was about to begin warming up his magnificent Loon singing voice, when Lolly and Fran called out in unison, "Look over there!!   Isn't that the highest peak of the 'Mountains of the Moon'!!"

And Lance, the most renowned geographer residing in our barely-moving-along barge jerked his head down, stared in the direction they were looking and cried out, "By Jove, you're right. It is the promontory of the highest of the Mountains of the Moon!!" [ed. note: It was the same mountain range, which much, much later was also described by Ptolemy. One wonders how he discovered it or whether its whereabouts had been known for eons, and he was just the first to describe it. The highest peak of that small mountain range is currently around 16,700 feet, but like Mt. Ararat at that time, it, too, was undergoing continuous uplifting movements. At the time of this sighting, Glenda and Carl estimated it to be around 13,780 feet high, making it the highest peak of that era.]

Quickly, Stan ran down the ramps to find me; once he did, we agreed I would locate Noah and have both of us immediately come up to the top deck. But even with repeated attempts, I couldn't get him to divulge what it was he wanted us to see. The only thing I could get out of him was, for once, it wasn't an emergency.

And as soon as Noah and I arrived at their viewing station, we both were struck by the awesome sight of seeing land jutting above the ocean swells that slowly swept us along. We estimated it to be approximately 20-30 miles east of us.

The significance of it being sighted didn't escape Noah *or me, for once*. He sighed deeply, while turning to me, and said, "That's a wonderful sign, Merrill. It means that the water level may be lowering. But for some reason it appears we will not be docking there. My guess is that the reason we aren't is that the land surrounding it would not be habitable for years, that it will remain wet and marsh-like, unable to provide us the minimum food sources that we have to have for any chance of survival. I have to guess that we are eventually going to dock in what used to be a drier climate, further away from the rain belt of the equator. After all, we are only about 160 miles from the equator at this point. But, at least we know the water level has either dropped or that it wasn't necessary to flood over that last peak we see in the distance. I'm encouraged, Merrill. None of us know what lies in front of us, but I take this as a hopeful sign. Go inform all the occupants in the regional compartments to come up and view this sight. Who knows? It may be the last land we see for a while."

And was he right in that prediction. But the evening was filled with a muted sort of gaiety with this sighting. And it gave Holly and me a chance to have a long chat with our dear friends, Lolly, Lance, Stan and Fran.

Archie, bless his heart, later asked Noah if he would like him and Alice to make a quick reconnaissance of that mountain's exposed peak the next morning. Noah was delighted to have them volunteer; it was nothing he'd ever ask someone to do.

And the next morning, they did fly over and were able to land on its surface. Their report, however, was neither altogether cheerful nor hopeful. There was no life found near or on top of the exposed surface. They searched everywhere and found none. If, in fact, this was the highest point on the planet's surface at that time, it did not harbor any survivors. But at least it was dry land; that alone gave us all hope. Archie's band were the last ones to be saved.

During the next 30 days, the routines on board Noah's ark were well established and a modest amount of peace reigned; or at least those of us in the more public positions thought so. But we were wrong. There was discontent and mounting anger fomenting on the second deck, amongst a few of the larger animals.

And nothing travels faster than discord, not even the speed of light. Just get self-righteous feelings of entitlement simmering, and before long you've got what we had coming to a full boil: a ready-to-serve mutiny.

It all came to light when Olive and Graham came to me the morning of May 16th, as I was finishing writing the previous day's watches on the wall log in the Wheel House. Olive spoke first.

"Merrill," she called out, as I exited and closed the Wheel House door, "we have a problem that has reached mutinous proportions, and we need you and Noah to call a boat-wide meeting today!"

"Why? Olive," I replied, stunned at her and Graham standing so resolute and determined before me. "What is going on?"

"It involves the wooly mammoths and saber tooth tigers," Graham began. "They have been fomenting trouble since this voyage began, and now it looks as if they are going to attempt a takeover of the entire boat."

"How did this all start?" I asked in amazement.

"Simply with bullying at first," Olive replied. "Initially, they wanted more room for themselves on the second deck. Due to the mammoth's huge bulk, they felt entitled to more room than what was assigned them. And the saber tooths simply wanted their neighbors further out of their way. They want completely free reign over their particular loft area. And both parties have extremely short tempers. Also, they want all the larger birds assigned to that area to be evicted. One of the saber tooths even threatened to eat one of the ostriches yesterday.

"Then the shakedown began. They felt they were not getting enough food and wanted more and more. Others began giving them portions of their own meager rations. Then came the protection scheme, whereby they made others around them do errands to keep from being harmed. They became crime bosses.

"Now, without any further delay, we must respond to protect the less powerful and innocent on that deck."

"Call a meeting of everyone for 11 a.m. this morning," I instructed them. "I will notify Noah and his family of the seriousness of the situation. Likewise, I need you to get Lewis and Lois, Elliot and Elaine and all the other larger cats, rhinos, hippos, bisons and buffalos together here on the top deck at 9:30 a.m. sharp. We need to discuss and plan how to ensure security for everyone, and what actions Noah's family decides to take to resolve this emerging problem. Thank you both so much for telling me. And Graham, Noah and I will probably have you Chair this 11 o'clock meeting, also on the top deck. Everyone on board must be told to be in attendance. Is that ok with you?"

"Absolutely," was all he said, straightening up to his full length, displaying his magnificent silver and grey mane and the rippling musculature throughout his torso and arms. I had the feeling he and Olive were ready to do battle, if that was what was required.

After my informing Nora and Noah of the pending meeting and the reason for it, they heartily agreed and began working out contingency plans for whatever direction this crisis might head. Given the size and ferocity of the parties involved, there was no limit to the chaos and harm that could come from circumstances becoming completely unmanageable. The bulk alone of the mammoths could do great damage to our boat, to the extent that it could be sunk. And the unpredictable behavior of the saber tooths could result in the serious injury or death of countless members of our shipmates.

It was only after some intense discussion within Noah's family that he finally came to me and said what they wanted done. Basically, the plan was to have Elliot, Elaine and the others who hefted the ramp up onto the top deck as The Storm began, to attach enough rope and harnesses onto the ramp again, after the ramp gate was opened, and have them maneuver it over the side of the ark about fifteen feet. Come 11 a.m. everyone would then encircle that gate opening, with Graham standing just in front of it. Immediately in front of him were to be the two mammoths and two saber tooth tigers, and immediately behind them would be the Guardians and other larger animals who could provide needed protection and force if events began to spiral out of control.

The procession of this upcoming assembly would be from the second deck downward, beginning with the larger animals, then the other regions behind them. Birds would have to find places to sit along the roofs of the Ramp House, Restroom Facilities and railings or simply circle overhead, if the deck area became too congested. Noah emphasized that everyone had to be there. It was probably to be a somber and sobering event. Already, the outcome seemed inevitable.

At 10:30 a.m. the Guardians and the others I had requested Olive and Graham to notify were to come, all assembled in front of Noah and his family members. Noah then advised them on how to proceed and reinforced that Graham would be in charge. It was not a matter of his shirking some responsibility, but more that of allowing a fellow creature's attempt to settle any dispute or issue the sentence if no peaceful remedy was found. Olive was to call the Assembly to order, and Graham was to conduct the Inquiry and pronounce any corrective actions or judgment.

And at 10:40 the procession began. The four malcontents were told that a boat-wide meeting had been called to address their concerns. And that the larger animals were to be seated at the front of the audience. Interestingly, because their egos had become more and more inflated, there was not the suspicion one might expect in such a situation. It was almost as if these four troublemakers anticipated that their actions and intimidations over these past weeks were about to bear fruit. They were to be anointed the leaders.

How sobering it is to see how blind ambition and corruption can transform someone. It made me glad to know that I was essentially a goofus.

And by 10:55 all the humans, animals and birds had gathered, perched or were hovering overhead that now still and breathless ark. The mammoths and saber tooths were finally positioned in front, and the Guardians quietly maneuvered themselves behind them. Olive then called the meeting to order.

"It has been noted over these last weeks, actually ever since this remarkably sad voyage began, that there were a few amongst us who have schemed tirelessly to bully, intimidate and threaten their way into a dominant leadership role over this vessel. They have essentially been working diligently to start a mutiny. And today is the response to their efforts.

"There has already been far too much ugliness perpetrated against this world's living creatures prior to our entering this boat, and most, if not all of it, has been at the hands of humans, with the significant exception of Nora and Noah and their families. Our hope leading up to our boarding this vessel that tragic day in February was that we would be leaving behind all that horror and waste.

But we didn't. It has followed us.

"And to outline this development in some detail and address what can be done to correct it, I will now let Graham come forward and speak to us."

Shocked at how this meeting was beginning, Holly and I, positioned at the front of this spectacle, toward the bow, couldn't help but notice some anxious shifting of position and turning of heads of both the mammoths and the saber tooths. And as they became more nervous, the Guardians, linking behind and beside them, edged closer together and closer to them. A wall of containment was slowly being built.

Graham nodded toward Olive, as recognition of her introduction, but there were no other formalities or niceties. It wasn't the occasion for such, and Olive knew it.

"For too long," Graham began, "there have been countless numbers of you gathered here, who have suffered silently at the hands of the four individuals standing before me. Their methods of intimidation and threat reached across all the regional boundaries and included animals and birds alike. There was not anyone on Deck #2 who was not affected or aware in some manner of their actions. But given the mandate by Noah that we should be slow to anger and always explore ways to compromise or excuse, each of us turned our attention elsewhere rather than confront four monsters that were growing daily within our midst.

"Now the time has come to confront these bullies before me and say 'no more' and 'not again'.

It is time to stop these two mammoths and saber tooths before a boat-wide upheaval ensues. Their ultimate plan, as we are all now beginning to see, is to set in motion a mutiny and then assume control of this vessel.

"And let me say, here and now, that is not going to happen!! And to stop their activities as of this moment, I am going to pronounce a sentence. No witnesses need to be called, no arguments need to be heard and no evidence needs to be presented. There is not anyone aboard this ark who is not aware of what we are addressing this morning.

"My judgment and that of all gathered here is that you four are guilty of plotting mutiny and of causing untold pain and discomfort since the beginning of this fateful voyage. And my sentence is that you four shall remain shackled in your quarters, in a twenty foot by twenty foot area, which will be cordoned off. And you will remain there until we disembark. Furthermore...."

But Graham was not able to finish his sentence, because at that moment there was a tremendous series of roars and, like serpents striking out at a prey, the two saber tooth tigers bounded towards Graham, obviously with the intention of mauling him. But unlike anything any of us had ever seen before, Graham demonstrated his physical grace and agility by crouching and then jumping high over their onrushing, lower-profile bodies. No sooner had they reached where he was standing seconds before, than he was now sailing over the top of them and landing facing the now onrushing mammoths. And just as nimbly, he darted to one side, doing a tuck and roll as he did, thereby missing their oncoming charge, roaring as they did. However, the momentum of all four, due to their uncontrollable rage and desire for revenge, carried them too far out onto the ramp that was jutting out over the edge of the boat. Before any of them could stop, they had cascaded out into space and into the ocean, forty feet below the top deck. And even with the tigers' ability to swim, the swells immediately began sweeping them further and further out into the distance. The mammoths disappeared almost as soon as they hit the water. [ed. note: Consider this the first recorded instance of Walking the Plank, but in this case it was more like Running the Plank.]

There were no shouts of joy or relief at this sudden, very dramatic change in what Noah, the Guardians and I thought was going to happen. No one in the audience on the top deck or circling overhead cheered. We had experienced far too much loss for that response. Inadvertently and impulsively, these four magnificent animals had doomed themselves and their offspring any chance of survival. Their two species were now to become extinct. [ed note: And you thought it had something to do with "tar pits".]

The gathering that day broke up with no celebration, although I have to be honest, there was some relief amongst a few of us. We were prepared to try to contain and control them, but we knew it was not going to be easy or maybe even possible. Later that day I thanked Olive and Graham for their courage and leadership. I understand Noah did the same soon afterward. Holly's and my respect for and trust of these two grew daily.

After that near-catastrophic, but ultimately, tragic episode, the next two months passed without incident. Shipboard life followed a very predictable routine. You could almost say it became a little boring, but that ended mid-morning, the day of my twelfth scheduled Watch, on our 142nd day at sea.

As I settled down to sit in the raised chair Ham and Japheth had recently constructed, which was secured behind the Ship's Wheel and enabled the individual on Watch to look out our one window into the distant horizon, I noted immediately something that was totally different from anything anyone had described to me before. In the distance was a large accumulation of dense, black clouds, rising high into the sky. But underneath them was an even darker horizontal line, beginning, I guessed, about five hundred feet above the water's surface and extending all the way across the ocean in front of me. And underneath it was an ominously, almost pure white bank of rolling clouds. And it was all heading straight for us. [ed. note: Think "white squall".]

Before I could do anything or alert anyone, the wind began gusting. All I could think was that we were about to experience another forty days and forty nights of this stormy weather again. But it was different this time. Rather than this clunky barge just bobbing along like it did in The Storm, this time it pitched and rolled terribly. And it began to veer off-course. The way I knew that was because Japheth had mounted the wooden box, with our rudimentary, pointer bowl inside it, to the Ship's Wheel pedestal. And he was able to place it in the exact middle of the front deck and our one window, with a bright white, caulk line pointing North, marked along the floor, up the wall and onto the window ledge. It made it easy to see that we were always heading in the 12° North by Northeast direction. But as soon as that storm hit us full-force, we were blown off-course and were tilting dangerously back and forth. I could only imagine what chaos was going on down below. There was no way this excuse-for-an-ocean-going-boat could withstand this pounding and we were being blown far off course, if the one we had been on all along was supposed to stay the same. *That was always a worry for us anyway. Where the heck were we going?* But I could only think that it was prearranged somehow and that the 12° heading was the one we had to keep, if we were ever diverted.

Becoming so very frightened by all the noise, the boat's lurching and bucking, along with our heading being completely detoured, I cried into the emptiness of the Wheel House, "Please... please." I didn't know what else to do or wail. It was not out of a concern for my safety, as much as it was for Holly's and all the precious friends and associates, who no doubt were being swept back and forth below me. "Please," I cried out repeatedly.

And then two events occurred, which forever changed me. The first was that there seemed to be a gradual lessening of the boat's heaving and twisting. And this continued to occur, even with the storm not losing its appearance or momentum, as it surged around us. We appeared to become sheltered in a kind of bubble. However, whatever happened, it didn't entirely buffer the storm's effects, but I didn't have the raw fear that our boat was about to capsize and all non-aquatic life would disappear forever.

And the second, and even more stunning, event happened immediately thereafter; and it was related to that silly Ship's Wheel that we had made and installed, primarily for Noah's benefit and pleasure. It not being attached to anything other than the pedestal, made it inert and impotent. It was basically a toy wheel, but each of us enjoyed sitting behind it, almost as much as Noah did. You just twisted and turned it at will, with nothing obviously happening. Until that day.

My hands had been holding that same Wheel, frozen motionless in fear, while I called out to the heavens for mercy and help. And after my outcry and noticing the diminished thrashing of our boat, I unconsciously turned the Wheel, like any one would do out of habit or as a displacement activity. But when I did, there wasn't the free play as always before. It had a resistance to my movement. I had to actually grab and apply force to the outside, wooden knobs to turn it.

And when I did that, looking down at the compass, the caulk line was now lined up with our heading being 280° West by Northwest. Gradually, as I turned the Ship's Wheel, straining as I did, I observed the heading changing to 285°, 290°, 300° and on and on like that over the next hour until I got the heading back onto the 12° North by Northeast. I had no idea if what I was doing was actually making any difference to the direction our craft was then taking or whether it was just my imagination. There were no reference points outside the window to tell me our direction was actually changing as I turned the Ship's Wheel, but for the remainder of my shift, until the storm passed, I was able to hold that course, even when gusts of wind surged around us. I truly felt something had happened that allowed me to steer our rudderless, bark-covered, life-raft. And it was confirmed later that same day around noon when Noah braved the storm and came up to see how I was doing. Within seconds of his grabbing the Wheel, at my request, he knew something wondrous had occurred, and I remember him saying one of his many prayers.

*Certainly, whatever happened that stormy day cannot be explained by me in any rational way. But it was an actual event, not an illusion, nor a swoon-like experience or me being overcome by some imaginary force. And why should humans be the only living creatures who experience such moments? I know it is not acceptable in places where theological discussions and supplicants gather for religious ceremonies to have animals or birds claim to have known and been touched by the very **Ultimate** of existence. But I did that night.*

And the only way I can explain it, even after all the nautical miles we traveled further from that spot, along with the months and years of transcribing and editing what took place in those times with Nora and Noah, was that it was real.

*And the only response I can give back to **Whoever** or **Whatever** intervened that day was one of thanksgiving and worship. And I could never, in all the days remaining in my life, describe **Who** or **What** came into my midst that same day. It was a majestic and awesome **Mystery,** far beyond my understanding.*

But I'm also sure that there will follow us - if life is allowed to continue beyond our small, but brave band of survivors - theologians, skeptics, philosophers and scientists who will spend a lifetime attempting to do so. And it is probably right that they should. But for me, it can only be explained as an event that was real; that the actions taken for the benefit of our scared and huddled collection of terrestrial life were concrete, visible and absolutely unexplainable except in terms of their being a Gift from the Heavens. Like The Storm we experienced for forty days and nights, this second one was also a Heavenly Warning. Both have to be held in awe and even feared. There is an innate weakness in humans, we animals and birds see that daily. But there can be a beauty and grace as well.

*My plea at this writing is that we admonish one another to recognize and respect the **Unknown** and **Unknowable** about us. By doing so, we will, in turn, be blessed with knowledge and calm that can only come from accepting it as such. This ark, if you will, stopped its violent rocking and pitching and was able, mysteriously, to be steered by a useless and silly Ship's Wheel by an **All-Present** and **All-Loving Hand**. My calls of "Please!...*

*please!", along with "Don't rock... the Boat!",
became prayers, not shouts, and they were
answered, not by the passengers aboard this bark-
covered excuse for a boat, but by a promise.*

*It was a promise filled with hope that life
will be possible for each of us in the future; with
faith that goodness will somehow prevail and with a
reassurance that there is a most-mysterious, yet
compassionate and everlasting **Deity**. Others who
follow us will, no doubt, clarify, enhance and
experience what I did that night and more ably
describe this Divination.*

*For me, it was transforming and humbling...
as if I had to be any more so. Being a meerkat does
not afford you many opportunities to feel elevated
above your status at being on the lowest rung on the
"food chain". But since that transformation, I have
never been the same. I was, if you will grant me
permission to utter it, touched by **The Holy**.*

DOCKING

SEVENTEEN: COPING WITH THE MANY STRESSES

There was some fallout from the tragedy surrounding the deaths of the four mutineers, and it was Graham and Olive who suffered most from it. It took many weeks for our Voyage Committee members to reassure and comfort them enough that they were finally able to accept that they had no responsibility in that day's sudden turn of events. While it was true that Noah had ordered that the ramp should be extended out over the edge of the top deck, doing so was simply to allow both of them the added room to address the packed audience on the top deck that day. It served as a kind of stage. Unfortunately, its placement also became a plank, which served to escort them quickly into "Davy's' Locker". It was only after I had had the frightening experience during the squall and the miraculous change in the Ship Wheel's capacity that their mood elevated and their self-confidence returned. And it was none too soon.

Assisting in their eventual recovery was the dismaying discovery of multiple leaks along the walls and up through the floor cants of the fourth deck. This area had been submerged the entire voyage and now was proving it. And, most disturbing, we didn't have any idea how much longer we would be stuck in this ocean, so the fear of becoming swamped gripped all of us. As usual, it was Olive who suggested to Noah that most of us on board should form a relay-chain again and quickly remove all our stored supplies to the third deck, and also have the occupants of the fourth deck take up residence on the top one. There followed a hectic few days with everyone on board helping make these transfers. Doing so also meant that a portion of Nora and Noah's family quarters were going to become the new cafeteria. Supplies eventually were stored both in their second deck area, as well as on the third deck. But by removing everything possible from the lowest deck, it made our humble, sea-going haven more unstable. Our boat was now, along with everything else, top heavy. All we needed was a good gale or storm front to come through and we'd keel over for sure. We were now sailing aboard a cork.

Amazingly, we did not lose any foodstuffs. Some of the plants got saturated, but they seemed to respond to the increased humidity, even if it was a bit salty. Likewise, the fourth deck occupants were thrilled to be able to sleep on the top deck. That said, however, the truly great fortune for everyone onboard, was that the leaking did not increase exponentially until just before we reached our final destination.

On July 17, a date that would mark the lessening of our mounting troubles, Noah spied a mountain top on the horizon, in the direct path of our 12° North by Northeast heading. He accidentally observed it during the waning hours of his shift, which, as it turned out, was to be our next to the last Watch on The Stretch. Mine would be the last, as it immediately followed his.

When I entered the Wheel House, Noah was sitting, as usual, on his Captain's Chair, behind the Ship's Wheel, steering our clunky hulk, as always, in that same direction. Indeed, it must be noted that over the last few weeks there had been a strong current running east to west, which would have drifted us far off course, if we hadn't had the amazing capability of steering this still- bark-covered excuse for a hotel.

As you can tell, by this time my patience was exhausted when it came to living on this poor excuse for a boat. But, little did I know at the time, we still had another 165 days to spend on it, even after we docked on the outcrop of rock immediately ahead of us.

"Look over here," Noah called to me, as I shut the door. Laying my staff against the table, I walked over nonchalantly, not expecting to see anything other than more water. "There's an outcrop of some kind straight ahead of us!" he exclaimed. "And it is in direct alignment with our heading, the one we've been on all this time. It must be our final destination! Praise **Yahweh**! We're nearly there!! I'll have to run down after my report and get Nora and the family. I want them to see this right away! Isn't it grand, Merrill!"

"Chief, it's the most welcome sight, ever, for these water-logged eyes. Would you please get Holly, as well, to come up here? My guess is that it's close enough that mine will be the last Watch, and she can be wakened for this glorious sight. Congratulations, boss! We made it at last!!"

"Here, grab the Wheel, Merrill. I'll give you my last report after a while. Let me run down right now and get everyone up here. Praise be!! We've nearly landed at our new home site, and we should be able to get off this ark pretty soon." *Little did he know, as well...*

The rest of my shift was spent with every creature on board coming forward to view the ever-expanding view of our final destination, as we maneuvered closer and closer. It appeared there was about two hundred feet elevation above sea level. And as I have already elucidated, the total height of that mountain was close to 13,680 feet above the previous water level that surrounded our world. Little did we know at the time that we had some months of waiting still ahead before we could set foot on terra firma, but at least this life-raft of ours would be on firm ground. After the last 190 days bobbling along and then experiencing increasingly more leaks inside the fourth deck area, it was an immense relief to at least dock her. By the time we actually docked there was a good two feet of water throughout the fourth deck, and it was filling faster and faster each day. The pitch and resin had held as long as they could. We were at our destination none too soon. Soon enough, the water level around us dropped below our keel line; and like the water had seeped in, it all eventually drained back out.

Complicating our lives, however, and making for even more hardship, was the announcement by Nora, after she, Tam, Kim, Tabeth and Holly did an inventory, that our food and water supplies were being depleted far too quickly. We had to begin rationing both.

From the time we landed on that mountain, which as it turned out was thankfully on an immense, level, outcrop of granite, we were faced with eating one meal a day... all of us. Not only that, but we only had enough water for one cup a day, which was not an issue for the birds, who shared their allotment with the larger animals. And we would have been even worse off if we hadn't had the penguins and pelicans doing their daily fishing to replenish our food stores. But, even that wasn't enough to prevent our beginning what was a long and tiresome period of semi-starvation for most of us. Fortunately, by now we were all the best of friends and bonded shipmates. It became a challenge we all met without complaint. *However, I must admit I did whine a bit to Holly from time to time about it all. But I never told you I was perfect, did I?*

Probably it was the combination of these two developments, our boat springing leaks which required relocating passengers to the top deck and the decreased food and water, which meant there were many of us up and about all hours of the night, resorting to eating the one meal nocturnally and sleeping during the daytime to combat thoughts of hunger and thirst, that saved us from our next crisis.

Why do I say that? Because we had our first and only onboard fire four weeks after we landed on the mountainside. And you will later be apprised of that event as well.

Once Noah had gone below and gotten Nora and their family members up on deck to see what now appeared to be our most likely destination, the word spread throughout the boat. It was a glorious moment. There were shouts of "land ho!" from every corner and deck. And the celebration of that sighting kept up until we got within a half mile of our destination. Then it dawned on Olive and Glenda that we had dangerously little in the way of maneuverability to dock our mammoth, floating, but now-slowly-sinking craft.

Running into the Wheel House, where I was still on Watch and nearly paralyzed with my hands frozen on the Ship's Wheel, Glenda shouted out as Olive threw open the door, "TURN SHARPLY TO PORT!!! You have to allow us to come in sideways!! If you don't, we'll crash headlong into that rocky peak!!"

Suddenly realizing the precariousness of our predicament, I began frantically turning the wheel, which even with that action, given the six hundred foot length of this bobbing, partially submerging bathtub, I knew nothing was going to happen quickly. And sure enough, there was a painfully slow process of the boat turning to port, which given our southern approach to this outcrop, meant we would eventually be facing west once we landed. Even then, I liked the idea of our facing into the setting sun, as evening approached, provided we could make a safe docking. What a tragedy it would be if after all our preparation, desperate departure and agonizing journey, we ended up shipwrecked and perishing on this ever-emerging mountainside.

"I'm turning as quickly as I can!" I shouted back to Glenda and Olive. And by this time Noah and Ham had run into the Wheel House, realizing what a challenge we had ahead of us to dock safely.

Blessedly, given our painfully slow rate of speed, our vessel did turn completely to the side, and we were nudged gracefully and gently onto the above-mentioned rocky shelf. And while, true there were a lot of scraping and grinding noises as we did, when it was all over, we were safely docked and upright. We had not crashed. And believe it or not, we were also on the level. How I knew that was once the noise stopped, I glanced down at our pointer box and saw that the sliver was still evenly balanced and indicated we were now pointed due west.

After the noise of docking completely subsided, there was a huge shout of relief from everyone. We had landed, at last. Our journey on "the Stretch" was over. Some of us cried, others cheered, and many prayed, as did I. At least this phase of our ordeal had ended. We couldn't even guess what now lay ahead of us, but we were too relieved to speculate at that moment. Soon enough I had to call a meeting of our Voyage Committee to initiate preliminary planning for disembarking. The Resettlement Committee would then have to be convened a few weeks after that. Finally, we were all beginning to see some finality to this never-ending tragedy.

But then, as I said, we experienced another near catastrophe: an onboard fire. That occurred on or around October 1st, and it coincided with our beginning to see the tops of other mountains surrounding this area, which was cause for some celebration, because it meant the water level was dropping considerably faster than we had anticipated. The atmosphere everywhere on the boat was charged with excitement, and it was time to have another party, which Paula organized handily. It was a smashing success, at least up until about 2 a.m. that next morning.

Everyone had partied so hard with dancing and singing that we all just collapsed on the top deck, the ramp into the second deck and throughout that area. Luckily for all of us, Elliot and Elaine had not made it past the Ramp House entrance. They bedded down with Holly and me next to the Wheel House. But everyone was awoken at that early morning hour with shouts of "Fire!! Fire!!"

Struggling to gain enough consciousness to sort out what was happening, I glanced over at our two pachyderm friends, who had already heaved themselves up off the deck surface and were lumbering through the still-awakening throng toward the smoke and fire.

The outdoor cook stove, similar to the one that Nora and her family used in their quarters, had been lit for the party. Water was boiled for tea around midnight and that was everyone's nightcap. But after we'd gone to bed, so to speak, apparently a rather strong breeze had come up, fanning the dying embers into a flow of sparks. Meanwhile, the tent covering the walkway to the Restroom Facilities had also been blowing loosely in that area. Combining these two events ignited the fire. Fortunately, the flames were going up toward the wooden roof covering the walkway. I say that, because had the fire reversed itself and reached the pitch-covered top deck, our life-saving boat would have become a funeral pyre.

And again, luckily, the large ceramic containers, in which we kept both drinking water for boiling the tea and salt water for keeping any fish caught by Archie and his companions before they were either cooked or dried, were still half full and near the fire's origin.

With moves so deft you hardly noticed them occurring, both Elliot and Elaine drew up that remaining water into their trunks and sprayed it repeatedly over the rapidly increasing area being engulfed by flames. Then others of us joined in with slapping the flames with wet rags. The two giraffes were able to slap the spreading fire as it neared the wooden roofline. And within a matter of minutes the flames were doused or extinguished. But it was too close to becoming another tragedy for all of us. The shouting and yelling didn't die down for some time following the smoke finally clearing. It scared everyone, including Noah. We had hoped and many of us had prayed that by then

our times of trial were about over. We were
completely exhausted.

EIGHTEEN: FINAL VOYAGE COMMITTEE MEETING

It had to be about the middle of October when I called the final meeting of the Voyage Committee. We had to finalize our last major assignment: preparing for our departure from this bloated barge...

I'm sorry, but by this time the romance was gone. I didn't care if I never saw another body of water or anything that floated on it ever again. And because of this, Holly and I decided our goal was to find the most remote and driest area possible to spend the rest of our lives, once we left there.

Because we were no longer staffing the Wheel House for watches, I instructed the Committee members to meet there at 9:30 a.m. that day. But you probably need to know that even though there were no longer watch reports to log, I still, and most probably out of habit, noted for each day any unusual or noteworthy event on the interior walls of the Wheel House. I later thought that we had better be leaving this beached tub sometime soon or I'd run out of room to record anything. But wishing didn't make it so. We still had more "hard time" to do.

It was Olive who called the meeting to order and exactly on time. Noah and Nora had just rushed in and sat down when she did. Displaying the politeness that we had all grown so accustomed to seeing throughout the voyage, she then asked if there were any other business items that needed to be added to her or my agenda before we got underway.

Nora spoke up immediately and requested some time to discuss the issue of our continuing need to ration food and water. She acknowledged that by our doing so up until then had markedly slowed the decline in our reserves, but we had to persist in doing so. And Noah suggested we give some thought as to how we would determine when the flood waters had receded sufficiently to begin offloading the ark of people, animals, birds and supplies. Graham was concerned, as always, about our being fair to everyone in deciding how and when the exiting process would proceed.

After their comments, Olive turned the meeting over to Glenda, who with Carl, had been working on a couple of issues for that day's meeting. Glenda began with, "We need to discuss the matter of how everyone is going to transport whatever supplies each region takes with them when we leave here. In addition, we have to determine the amount each group is taking.

"As a preliminary suggestion, Carl and I, in conference with Nora, recommend we begin this discussion with each of the five regions having four carts, while Nora and Noah's individual families have one cart each, for a total of twenty-four carts that would have to be constructed in the time remaining before our departure."

"How do you propose we construct them and with what?" Noah quickly interjected. "It's not like we have a lot of extra material lying about."

Carl then spoke up. "We determined that if we dismantled the wooden roof over the partially tented walkway from the Ramp House to the Restroom Facilities that there will be enough wood to fashion wheels and carts. The attached axles and tongues to pull them along can be constructed by shaping-to-size some roost poles suspended over Deck #4. Any tack for pulling them will have to be fashioned from the ropes and harnesses we have made for pulling up and lowering the ramp that is still in position on our top deck. And as far as the design goes, they would have to be two-wheeled carts; there is not enough wood to make them any larger. I would estimate the wheels would be three feet in diameter and the cart itself would be six feet wide by eight feet long and five feet deep. They would not be for carrying passengers; they are for supplies only."

"Who would build them?" Nora asked, her voice indicating some amazement at how much thought had already been given this matter.

"Any of us animals who could, would lend a hand, at least in the dismantling of the roof section and shifting around any building materials. But, I'm afraid the actual building would fall on Ham, Shem, Japheth and their families. And I would propose, if this suggestion is accepted, that they should begin right away. The rate at which the water level is falling seems to indicate that we will be able to leave here in just a few months' time."

With great relief in his voice, Noah then offered, "I would suggest that we vote to approve this idea and begin dismantling the roof and construction of the carts immediately. Do I hear a second?"

"I second," I added quickly.

"Then it's decided," Olive concluded. "Now on to the next item, supply distribution."

Nora spoke up at that point, "I would suggest that Holly, Tam, Kim and I begin the process of inventorying all stored supplies, ones that were set aside for our post-voyage journey over land. And we will set them in six different sections of our families' quarters. That will allow anyone the opportunity to see how the supplies have been allocated. Unlike the birds and animals, who will be able to forage, at least to some extent, along the way, our families will be more dependent on what we have brought along with us. I worry that our ultimate survival will hinge on how well we manage these meager supplies during that journey to wherever we all eventually settle."

Graham spoke up at this point, saying "That's fair enough. We will have a boat-wide meeting in a month or so and discuss all this and outline the issue of how the supplies are to be divided up. Certainly, all of us hope that there will have been enough time for some regrowth and repair of some species of grasses and trees after all this flooding. I know for certain, everyone, including those of us sitting here, are extremely anxious to be on our way, as soon as we get the signal to do so. And certainly we want everyone to leave here feeling like their survival has been given the fairest consideration that the circumstances would allow."

"Good," Olive chimed in. "Then that's settled. Everyone should begin these projects today. Now, I have another issue about our departure. How do we stage it?"

At this point I spoke up again. "I believe the regions that had to exist in the lowest portion of this boat should leave first. They have endured the most hardship. And as each region leaves, I'd like them to take a moment to tie their neck ribbons on the railing surrounding the top deck. Once they are attached, it will give this barge a modest, but colorful, farewell. And it should be an orderly exit, with each region's carts proceeded down the ramp with them. The larger animals of those regions, the ones that have been bunked on the second deck, will accompany them at that time, and of course they will be expected to share in pulling the carts."

To my suggestions, everyone simply nodded their heads in agreement.

"Now then, is there any other topic that we should discuss?" Olive added. "Noah, didn't you want to discuss the manner of our determining how we will know when it is time to begin our evacuations?"

"Yes, I did," he replied. "And I was thinking that we should select a bird or two who

223

would fly off at a designated time and come back to report their findings."

"Who were you thinking would perform that task?" I asked.

"Well, I thought of a raven," he replied, to the absolute astonishment of all of us sitting there.

"A RAVEN!" I exclaimed. "We've got the most amazing collection of birdlife ever assembled in any one place, probably now and for all time to come; and you want a RAVEN to have that honor!! What about the Messengers, who spent those weeks and months getting the word out to everyone throughout the five corners of our planet? What about Stan, the stork. Or Lance or Lolly, the loons who did so much for us at the beginning? Or what about those birds who have serenaded us every evening with their haunting and glorious voices? A RAVEN, for Pete's sake!!"

My outburst caught everyone by surprise. As a rule, no one challenged Noah when he made a decision. And my outcry was not met with any nodding of heads, even if there was possibly some agreement with me.

"Yes, I have decided on a raven, despite your objections, Merrill," Noah added. And if having one of them go is not successful, I will then try a dove."

I hung my head in despair. *And I thought long and hard afterwards that the rewards one gets for their good works surely doesn't come at the moment they think it should. To my knowledge no raven or dove had done anything this entire voyage, or what preceded it, that I could recall. But they were the chosen scouts. If I could have sprouted wings at that moment, I think I would have gathered up Holly and bid everyone on board a safe rest of the journey. In my mind, I knew who had made this venture possible. And it sure wasn't any black bird or some whimpering dove. Holly calmed me down later that day, but I never forgot that snub. It just wasn't fair.*

Our Committee meeting broke up an hour later, with most everyone in agreement with what had been discussed and agreed upon. And for the next two weeks or so the work on the top deck was spell-binding. Everyone wanted to be involved in these final preparations. It boosted our morale to see it all unfolding. And then the decision was made to send out the two birds.

DEBARKATION

NINETEEN: BIRDS FLY AND FREEDOM COMES

And so, two weeks after that final Voyage Committee meeting, Noah, as promised, decided one early morning that it was time to see how dry the land was below them. To do so, he proceeded to instruct one of the ravens to fly out and check for him. And wouldn't you know, the bird never came back!! I told him, in so many words, that was what would happen. He didn't even come back to say, in answer to the question "What did you see?", "Not much." He just didn't say anything. Nada. He bugged off, and left us stranded on this mountain.

When that happened, Noah later sent one of the doves off to investigate what was below us. She did return, which I thought was mighty nice of her. The little that Noah confided to me, probably because he was well aware of my disapproval of the manner and the choice of scouts he was sending, was that she couldn't find a place to rest. In other words, there were no exposed forests or other vegetation to support her or give her sustenance. His quote to me was that she saw only "this and that".

Brilliant!! We worked and sweated over a year on this flood project, and the only scout that returned was inarticulate! The least Noah could have done was determine if this individual could talk in anything other than pithy phrases. By then, he knew full-well my disgust at it all.

But undeterred, he sent her out again one week later. This time she came back with an olive leaf in her mouth. And when I asked what she found, he said "not much", because she had her mouth filled with that leaf. *I stuck my finger down my throat and tried to gag myself...*

And to top it off, one week later, he did the same thing, and she, too, never returned. Two batters up; two strike outs. And I guessed we were supposed to theorize what their not returning was supposed to mean. I simply felt they bugged off. Noah took it as a great and mighty sign of some kind. It escaped me what kind of sign it was, because we still had another 98 days to wait until we could finally exit that overgrown lifeboat.

So, I began having Lolly, Lance and Stan do some unofficial scouting for a few of us. We had to begin to plan on a direction to travel once we were finally able to leave the boat. It wasn't enough to just wander off somewhere. We had to have a plan.

Another thing was becoming very clear to Holly and me. The weather was staying warm and very dry. It was as if the **Floodmaster** realized that we had to have this in order to eventually find our way and to have a chance of any long term survival. Glenda and Carl informed Holly and me that the seasons were reversed up here, above the equator, from what they were below it where we used to live. That being so, they noted that we should now be heading into the winter months. It was comforting to sense that we weren't going to have to endure the cold and snow that might have come under more ordinary circumstances. Not that there was anything ordinary about what we'd all experienced over these last eighteen months.

During the next three weeks, Noah and I kept our distance from one another. He was not pleased with my behavior; neither was Holly for that matter, and I was certainly not enamored with his decisions of late. But his birthday was coming up in another week or so, on January 1st. He was reported to then be 601 years old!! I didn't even know trees could be that old!! And Holly warned me to stay away from him, if I continued to have a testy attitude about him or his age. She warned me that I was approaching insufferable.

And deep down I even saw signs of it myself. I blamed it all on having a moderate case of "cabin fever". It was going around, even the birds that knew they could fly away, if there was somewhere to go, were experiencing it. I just needed to stretch my legs, run a few miles in a straight line, along a sandy outcrop of hills, see a fruit tree blossom, experience a horizon in which there was absolutely no water anywhere.

Knowing all that, I decided it was time to call the first and probably the only meeting of the

Relocation Committee. And because Holly and Noah were also on that committee, I thought it might serve as an opportunity for me to make amends with both of them... somehow. Japheth was still very busy with his other family members building the carts, but I hoped the meeting would not take too long. We met in the Wheel House at 10 a.m., during that third week in December, and I had Kyle call the meeting to order.

The unresolved issues that Kyle outlined for us were ensuring that everyone exited safely and orderly down the ramp, once the Ramp Gate was opened and the ramp was lowered to the ground. We sure didn't need a stampede at that moment. Next, the Committee needed to meet with Nora and her group and double-check the food and water supplies that had been set aside for each region to take with them. Likewise, we needed to insure that each region's self-appointed guide or leader had the appropriate heading that they were to take. After all, our recently completed voyage had no doubt disrupted everyone's usual internal migration patterns and pathways. Glenda and Carl worked out compass headings for each region to follow as they began their march back home. And finally, it was decided that Noah should say a few words to everyone on our last evening on this tub, before we all began our journeys to the far corners of this now uninhabited planet. It only seemed fitting that he should, and I seconded the motion when it came time to approve his doing so. He looked at me and smiled when I did, and after that our relationship began to warm again.

Then came January 1st. It was a day of surprises and celebration. Not only was it Noah's birthday, but the land, as far as we could see, was free of water! What had been a world mixed with gray to blue-green water was now a landscape covered with rich-looking, milk-chocolate colored soil. Not only was there no water; the earth was dry! No sign of moisture could be seen anywhere! And closest to us, where the rocky crags would allow the life-supporting soil to deposit, there were blades of grass beginning to sprout. It was the deepest green, like that seen when fields of early Spring alfalfa first appear. It looked like the finest textured woolen carpet, spread out below the deep blue sky and against the black granite mountain tops, which were scattered across the horizon. You couldn't take your eyes off the vista before you. It was like a visible prayer, not uttered in desperation or forlorn hope, but in response to suffering beyond anything imaginable. Certainly, we were to see the spectacular rainbows appear in the weeks and months to come, but for us creatures of the land, nothing compared to seeing our world's surface being returned to us intact and vibrant.

In addition, apparently Noah had recently been given the ok by the **Floodmaster** to begin disassembling the Ramp and Wheel Houses. There was no longer any need for covering the top deck. And it was a few days after this process began that Lewis and Lois came to Holly and I, as we were lounging in our sleeping quarters. It was Lois who spoke first.

"Good afternoon, Holly and Merrill," she

began. "Lewis, other members of the Guardians and I have been having some discussion about what is to happen once we are free to leave this marooned hulk." *Already, after hearing her say this, I was tuned in to whatever she was about to say. Her feelings toward this tub fit mine exactly.* "And we have a few suggestions to offer you. But it will entail the cooperation of Noah's family members to complete most of them."

"What is it exactly you are thinking about?" Holly asked, awakening slowly from a deep nap.

"We have seen the various carts being constructed, and note that most of them have been completed and stored on the old, fourth deck. We feel it is time now to build two more, larger ones; but each of these should have four wheels instead of two."

"How do you propose getting the wood to build them?" I asked, my curiosity now being aroused.

"From the material being dismantled from the Ramp House," Lewis replied. "And then once the two new carts are finished, the walls of the Wheel House can be loaded into them. And whatever room is left over can hold whatever few supplies remain after all the other carts have been filled."

"The reason for our suggesting this," Lois interrupted, "is because we know you both have been very diligent in writing down everything that has happened while we have been aboard this boat... of sorts. And we feel it is now extremely important that it be transferred to a safe place for you to finish your work in preserving what you inscribed on those walls for others to see, sometime in the future."

"Furthermore," Lewis added, excitedly, "We, and by 'we' I mean all of us who were Guardians, have voted and agreed to accompany you two and Noah's families to the areas where you choose to settle. We can help pull the various carts and wagons along the way. And then once you are safely settled, some of us may move on toward our previous homeland, and some of us may even stay on with you. My understanding right now is that Lolly, Lance, Fran and Stan are staying with you. They feel they can raise their new family there with you just as easily as anywhere else. The rest of us have a deep desire to return, at least to the African mainland to begin our lives again and to start our new families.

"So, what do you think about our offer?"

Holly and I stared at one another for a nerve-wracking moment and then broke out in loud, uninhibited cheering and laughter. We had been so worried about what was going to happen to us when it came time to leave this place. We anticipated we'd just have to stay on here to get the recording done. It had become an overwhelming and depressing concern for both of us. And now the answer, like to one of Noah's prayers, had come in the form of Lewis and Lois.

Reaching out to both of them and hugging them tightly, we shouted, "Of course, we'll do it. And thank you so very, very much for your friendship and loyalty."

After that conversation, and throughout the days that followed, the Guardians were very much involved in the dismantling of the two shelters on the top deck, with Elliot and Elaine carefully stacking the wooden siding of the Wheel House where it once stood. The pointer was given to Glenda and Carl. And there was enough chalk left for me to scribble down the last activities of our next few weeks and Noah's Commencement Address word-for-word to all of us. Then the day before we departed, all of us loaded the wood onto the two wagons that Ham and Shem had so carefully constructed from the Ramp House's roof and sides.

Next, the two-wheeled carts were brought up topside, and each filled with their respective region's supplies, seeds and plants stationed at the bow as well. From all appearances, and given the heightened sense of anticipation, by the evening of February 26th, everyone was packed, primed and ready to leave. And it was then that Noah and his family invited all of us to join them on the top deck for his farewell speech.

TWENTY: NOAH'S FAREWELL ADDRESS
AND OUR DEPARTURE

It was dusk; the sun having set and the first stars had yet to appear on the far horizon, that night of February 26th. All of us, Nora, Noah's sons and their wives and children, all the animals, birds and the smallest of creatures assembled in, on or about every exposed surface that the top deck provided. The railings, again, were filled with perched birds, as were the roofs of the Restroom Facilities. There were, by now, no other structures left standing. The ramp had been lowered earlier in the day, with all the ropes and harnesses reattached for the mighty effort it took by the largest of our animals to lift it up, then pull and shove it into place. And then the harnesses were removed from the ramp and attached to the various carts and wagons. Once that was done, the Ramp Gate was shut. No one was to leave Noah's ark until sunrise the next morning.

The top deck fire box was turned upside down in front of that gate, and Nora and Noah were helped up onto it by their sons and family. Once they were both on top, a hush came over all of us.

Only a slight breeze could be felt, but there were no gusts of wind, even at the altitude where we were marooned. Then Nora spoke first.

"Family members and fellow travelers, all of whom have become such close and dear friends to Noah and me, welcome to this final gathering in one place of all life on this planet. Never before has there been such an event and never again will it reoccur. It was the greatest honor for me to be associated with and gotten to know all of you over these almost two years. Aside from the only disturbing event involving four of our members a few months ago, each of you have endured the indescribable hardships and shown remarkable bravery, with utmost faith in Noah, myself and our **God**. You trusted us. You had a faith, not out of understanding or wisdom, but out of the purest of trust and faith in a **God, Whose** mercy will soon replace the utter decimation of all life that we have witnessed. Never will I be able to comprehend the effort it took for you to come to that belief. It, above all else, shows the commitment to life that exists within each of you. You didn't rock the boat, and I am sure you never will. You are the bedrock of life on this world. And Noah and I salute you and will love you all until our last breath. Thank you for the honor of being able to live and work amongst you. And have a safe journey and a fruitful life beyond this small world we will soon leave. You, at the very least, deserve that. Farewell, my dear friends."

Immediately, after she finished her little speech, the roar that rose out of our throats was heard for miles across those mountains. If landslides had been started, if would not have surprised me. The roaring undulated, shifting in tone and volume, but kept up for at least five uninterrupted minutes. It was the only way we knew how to salute her. Our affection for her was unmistakable. In response, she bowed repeatedly and blew kisses in every direction. As I have said elsewhere, short of Holly, I would have easily lived with Nora the rest of my days in complete bliss.

Then Noah rose from the bench that had been set on the box for each of them to use when the other was speaking. Despite the staggering age that he was reported to be, he still stood amazingly erect and moved with a quickness of a much, much, younger man.

Clearing his throat, after sweeping his head to look around and above him, he finally spoke.

"Nora, my family members and all of you most precious, dear friends and fellow survivors, I want to try and express my deepest and most heart-felt gratitude for what you have endured so bravely and without complaint. There is no victory to celebrate tonight. No conquest was made by your noble efforts. Nothing that has occurred over these last two years can be honored, other than your courage and willingness to sacrifice everything.

"We have each lost so much. Nora and I still have our immediate family intact, but at that we still did lose countless relatives in The Flood. But for each of you, the personal losses were much more extensive. If it were my place, I would offer the most profound apology for all your losses; but like you, I was only another drafted participant in the most tragic event of what is now called 'prehistory'. We can only hope that one day, with Holly and Merrill's recording what we've been through, that our losses and toils will become a part of history. And then, at that moment, when their writings are exposed to the light of some contemporary society, it will all be seen as an event unequaled in all the history of recorded life.

"For sure, there will be or already have been extinction events spread across this world, but none will ever match the sweep of death that we were witness to. And may **God** have mercy on everything and everyone if there should ever be another one, anywhere approaching the magnitude of what we've just experienced. And it is to that point that I would like to address the rest of my remarks tonight. However, nothing I say here approaches the feeling of thankfulness that I feel toward each of you for sheltering alongside Nora and my family all these past months.

"What led to this indescribable Flood? How could something approaching its magnitude ever happen again? There is no way I can truthfully answer these questions, but I do want it eventually recorded that we at least tried to warn others about what seemed to precede The Event we've just experienced.

"With us - and it was the people of this world that certainly were the culprits in causing this ever-lasting tragedy - it all began innocently enough. We simply became careless. It began with careless thinking and imaginings. We let our minds wander aimlessly into realms that would eventually lead to subtle acts of dishonest disregard for others. The carelessness became habitual, whether it was of a personal nature or it extended beyond into dealings with neighboring tribes, groups of communities, belief systems and finally entire regional or national ruling bodies. It was sinister how it seeped into the fabric of everything, allowing time for everyone to justify whatever they did, no matter how harmful it might become.

"And this pervasive behavior was followed by our world becoming more and more at risk. The carelessness careened out of control. To compensate for one act of harm, we would fabricate another act equally harmful but less obvious. Before we knew it, we were risking our happiness, security, welfare and very existence. It was so insidious at first, this risky state of things. And yet, there was still time to reverse the course of events, if everyone recognized their selfish behavior and began acting in concert to protect and, most importantly, be merciful with and to one another.

"Mark this. Showing mercy is the most trustworthy sign that an individual, group or regional body is on the road to recovery from a selfish and careless lifestyle. Living by the so-called 'Golden Rule' will not do it. 'Doing unto others as I would have them do unto me' was not going to combat the pervasive contagion that gripped the people of this world before The Flood. The careless behavior patterns that became the norm changed the very soul of that admonition.

"The only measure that can be used, in

every circumstance, in any time, is the ability and willingness of a person or a people to show others mercy. More than hope, faith and even the overt expressions of love, to demonstrate mercy says all of that in the most sincere and unquestionable way. There is then no doubt what motivates any individual or society. Without mercy, and the thoughtfulness and careful attention that accompany it, carelessness abounds, and this world will suffer a similar event as we have just experienced. And mark my words; there will ultimately be another flood-like event if care is not taken.

"We have left behind simpler times. The Flood and its destruction have altered forever our vision of ourselves and the world around us. There is nothing to celebrate about what has just happened to us. But we must remember. This Event cannot be forgotten or lost in the recesses of time. The chance of our world again being capsized in greed and lustful power is never going to be completely lessened, if enough choose to become careless.

"I urge you now to face each day with a renewed hope and commitment. Heaven knows, you deserve the former, and so much more; while at the same time, we each must strive for the latter. You were simply the victims in this tragedy; we were the perpetrators of it all. Tomorrow, February 27th, will never be a day set aside on anyone's calendar. There will be no flags waving, banners flying, bands playing or parades passing by to mark this day. But each of us must remember. And we must teach those who follow us to remember: not a particular day but a way of life, an outlook, a constant vigilance to not become lost. Our duty from this moment on is to help others find their way, to keep from becoming lost and to be merciful to one another. And at the core of all that to help them find a **God** that is **Love**, is **Merciful** and wants for each of us a life everlasting.

"And, again, Nora, my family and I thank you with all the energy left in us this night for being such a brave and wondrous band. You didn't rock the boat, as Merrill worried so about. You kept it straight on course. You are true navigators of goodness and may **God** bless each of you assembled in this place tonight. Farewell, my friends."

Needless to say, following his address, there was silence for a few moments, but then the low mummer of pride in a job well done and of someone who had given them the ultimate salute began to swell. Soon there was a roar heard across the length and breadth of the world at that time. It was one which emanated from the depths of every creature on board that soon-to-be abandoned ark, including Nora, Noah and his family. We all raised our heads and yelled to the heavens. It was not just a joyous sound. More than that, it was a way of recording that we were there and that this was the beginning of the second beginning.

Few, if any of us, slept at all that same night, in anticipation of what the morning would bring: our freedom from the confines of this place. It wasn't like we had been up celebrating, like it was New Year's or some other holiday; it was, most likely, from anxiety. What would we see? How easy would our travels be? What obstacles would slow us down or maybe even prevent any of us from getting back to our homes? And, most of all, we worried 'would we be able to find enough food and water?' Why? Because our rations had become pitifully depleted; we had not anticipated we would be confined this long on Noah's ark.

Just the same, like any soldiers primed and given their orders and the directions to head, by first light the ramps throughout the boat were filled with the first region to leave; it was Australia, the smallest contingent. As they filed to the now-open Ramp Gate, Nora, Noah and all their family, along with Holly and the Guardians, Lolly, Lance, Fran and Stan stood at attention saluting them each one as they filed down the ramp. The carts, previously set aside on the bow side of the top deck, had been arranged in order so that as each body of countries would depart, they could pick them up. The above Honor Guard stood on the stern side of the top deck. And me? With staff in hand, I led the way for that first group to file down and head off into the New World below us.

Once I descended down the ramp, each cart of a respective region came first, and then that area's animals and birds followed. No birds flew off that morning. They all passed in review, walking or hopping as they did. It was one of the most moving sights any of us ever experienced. Maybe **Someone** or Some Unseen Legion of Hosts were cheering and waving, but none of us did that day. It was too awe-inspiring an event for any of us to voice any sound. There was a dignity and solemnity in that procession that warranted the greatest respect and quiet. Life was leaving this Ark of Noah's and it was about to replenish the earth, devoid of any up until then.

Prior to the first group's leaving, they tied their neck ribbons, most very tattered and well worn onto the deck's railing. And as they filed through the Ramp Gate, the next region's representatives did the same, and so the process went until all the boat's railings were filled with the colors of all five continental groups. It gave the aging, stranded boat an appearance of significance and worth. And as we each turned around and looked back at her, as we all filed down Mt. Ararat's gradual sloping sides, she appeared proud and satisfied. Her job was done.

One by one each region passed in review, until it was time for our group, who had been standing at attention the entire time, to attach the harnesses and grab onto ropes and begin easing our four carts and two wagons down the ramp. Interestingly, as the last of us left the top deck, Noah was the last to exit, and he made a point of closing and securing the Ramp Gate. I asked him later why he did, and he replied, "It seemed fitting. It was like closing the cover of a well-read book, or making the bed after a long and difficult night's slumber, or honoring a shelter that had somehow kept you safe in the most terrible of storms and times." I could only nod my head at his reply.

Each region, as I mentioned before, had been given instructions by Glenda and Carl as to the heading they were to take once they got off the boat.   And as our group began heading off the mountain shelf that we had been perched on, I surveyed the entire panorama around us. And sure enough, there were the five groups, with birds now flying immediately overhead each one, ambling off in all the cardinal directions, east, west, north and south. Our heading was to be south by southwest. It was estimated that we'd have to travel eight hundred miles before we arrived at the area where Noah's family wanted to resettle and where Holly and I could find a satisfactory place to begin rewriting the watch log, written on the Wheel House siding.

Our group's carts were pulled by Noah's sons and their sons, and the two wagons were pulled by the Guardians. Elliot and Elaine each took a separate wagon to begin the march. I would always take turns walking beside whoever was pulling the wagons, and I kept up a constant chatter as we walked. It was the least I felt I could do.

And the trip down the mountain was not as hazardous as we had anticipated. It was, at that moment, in a quiet and stable stage of growth. [ed. note: It apparently would not begin its renewed uplifting until many centuries later.] The sloping was gradual, not steep and filled with rocky crags that would tip over our carts and wagons. And the deep ravines had been filled with the silt and sand from The Flood waters. By the afternoon that same day, all five regions and our little band had made it successfully and safely to the bottom of the mountain.

Our group averaged 1-2 miles an hour, and

we walked ten hours a day. And oddly, as unbelievable as it seems, in forty days and nights...AGAIN...we had arrived at our destination. At least it was the one for some of us.

The place Nora and Noah chose was perfect. It was close to the ocean, and yet far enough back not to be in view and thereby revive old memories of our terrible ordeal. Eventually, as memories faded, they and their family could cast their nets upon it and catch enough fish to feed themselves indefinitely. The place for all their home sites had a lovely stream beginning to clear from all the silt recently deposited by The Flood. There was even grass beginning to grow tall enough for easy grazing by their cattle, goats and sheep. Woods were located nearby for some building material, but the surrounding rocky cliffs would provide most of the material needed for safe and sturdy buildings, once they were framed.

After getting them settled over the next five days, the Guardians, Lolly, Lance, Fran and Stan accompanied Holly and I over to our new homesite, which was on the other side of a high range of hills, just east of Nora and Noah's as before. We chose a cliff site, with caves already carved into many of the hillsides... hundreds of them. And below us were lush grasslands that stretched as far as the eye could see and a magnificent lake, the first we'd seen in our travels, since leaving Mt. Ararat.

[ed. note: Little did they know that this "lake" was eventually to be named "The Dead Sea", and it was to be the lowest and one of the driest places on the planet. Hence, it was the perfect spot to store these tablets, from which I have been translating this story. And the "lush" grasslands eventually turned into magnificent, ancient forests, which ultimately became the fermented ingredients for the world's biggest oil reserves. It's a shame Holly and Merrill couldn't have registered mineral rights to that region, and then passed them on to their ancestors... and me.]

It took them two weeks to unload and stack the wooden sides of the Wheel House in various rooms within these countless caves. They were stored in such a way that they could easily be brought into a well-lighted area for Holly and me to transfer the texts onto clay tablets.

The majority of the Guardians, immediately after helping us organize all this material and after they had had a chance to rest and revive their starved condition, chose to resume their trek further into Africa. It was a heart-wrenching moment to see them file off into the distance, the elephants setting the pace, with Lewis and Lois bringing up the rear to ensure no one was straggling due to exhaustion or thirst. Our good-byes were not prolonged, but they were deeply heartfelt. However anyone would choose to define the deepest of friendships, those beloved creatures were just such for Holly and I.

Staying with us for the remainder of all our lives were Lolly, Lance, Fran and Stan. We and they all began families soon thereafter and settled into a comfortable, but very busy lifestyle of preparing tablets, recording on them and then stacking them in chronological order in the furthest cave in our complex. It literally took us years to complete this project, but we all knew it had to be done.

But before I forget, there was one other pair of birds that stayed behind with us at our home site by the immense lake. They were the skylarks. For some reason they never made a sound the entire voyage or any time before or after it. It wasn't until we had finished our task of rewriting these testaments, that someone may find one day, that they did.

It was one beautiful Spring evening, when the sun had almost completely set behind us, and their shadows were beginning to sweep slowly out across the waters in front of us. There was a light breeze blowing, signaling a tide change was in progress over Nora and Noah's way. And not another sound was heard, not until we noticed overhead one of the skylarks beginning to make a circular climb into the sky. As he did, the most beautiful song began cascading downward, as he flew higher and higher in ever-widening circles. This went on for the duration of any daylight, and it was absolutely magical. We all sat there spellbound, looking and listening to this performance. And as he sang, a rainbow appeared on the eastern horizon, arching across the entire breadth of the visible sky. We knew, intuitively, that all this had to have a meaning far beyond a casual event. It was both a benediction and the sign of a promise or pledge to whoever came after us.

I couldn't help but excuse myself when all this magnificent performance and sight was concluded and go inside our residence and take up the last clay tablet that we had left. It was to have these final words about Noah and The Flood inscribed on it. And, in conclusion, I leave this for each of you:

"For all that is everlasting, beautiful and holy, anyone who should find and read this account, please take care. Take care with all that you think, with what you feel and even with what you do. Each, if abused, can lead to the worst kind of behavior, habits and sadness. And the damage that will result will not only affect you, but all those around you, not just the ones who love and cherish you. Reread what Holly and I have written here if you doubt me. But, **God** forbid, if for some reason, or for some brief moment you, whether as an individual, a people, a land or a world, should become careless or lost, remember each life's voyage is so precious and is always worth another launching... always.... always........ always."

EPILOGUE

TWENTY-ONE: THE PRESENT DAY...AGAIN

Who could add anything more to this record of Noah's ark?   I certainly can't.   But maybe for their sake I should, if only to say that at the very least this world certainly doesn't need another Noah-type flood again.   Maybe just a more localized baptismal event might help convince the unyielding and unwilling to alter their ways and to accept the uniqueness of all life and the need to allow freedom to exist in its almost hysterical manifestation at times.

From my perspective, humanity hasn't changed so much since those earliest times that Merrill and Holly described. It seems odd that that should be the case. Adaptive behavior to nurture, preserve and protect a species is present in all other life forms. I have to wonder what it will take to convince the descendents of Nora and Noah that they should and must do the same.

Our boat seems to be rocking more violently with each passing day.

APPENDIX

THE OLD TESTAMENT'S GENESIS ARK STORY

Genesis 6: 5-22

"5 And God saw that the wickedness of man was great in the earth and that every imagination of the thoughts of his heart was only evil continually.

6 And it repented the Lord that he had made man on the earth, and it grieved him at his heart.

7 And the Lord said I will destroy man whom I have created from the face of the earth, both man and beast and the creeping thing, and the fowls of the air. For it repenteth me that I have made them.

8 But Noah found grace in the eyes of the Lord.

9 These are the generations of Noah. Noah was a just man and perfect in his generations, and Noah walked with God.

10 And begat three sons, Shem, Ham, Japheth.

11 The earth was also corrupt before God, and the earth was also filled with violence.

12 And God looked upon the earth, and behold it was corrupt; for all flesh had corrupted his way upon the earth.

13 And God said unto Noah, The end of all flesh is come before me. For the earth is filled with violence through them, and behold I will destroy them with the earth.

14 Make thee an ark of gopher wood; rooms shalt thou make in the ark, and shalt pitch it within and without with pitch.

15 And this is the fashion which thou shall make it of: the length of the ark shall be three hundred cubits, the breadth of it fifty cubits, and the height of it thirty cubits.

16 A window shalt thou make to the ark, and in a cubit shall thou finish it above; and the door of the ark shalt thou set in the side thereof; with lower, second, and third stories shalt thou make it.

17 And, behold, I, even I, do bring a flood of waters upon the earth, to destroy all flesh, wherein is the breath of life, from under heaven; and every thing that is in the earth shall die.

18 But with thee will I establish my covenant; and thou shalt come into the ark, thou, and thy sons, and thy wife, and thy sons' wives with thee.

19 And of every living thing of all flesh, two of every sort shalt thou bring into the ark, to keep them alive with thee; they shall be male and female.

20 Of fowls after their kind, and of cattle after their kind, of every creeping thing of the earth after his kind, two of every sort shall come unto thee, to keep them alive.

21 And take thou unto thee of all food that is eaten, and thou shalt gather it to thee; and it shall be for food for thee, and for them.

22 Thus did Noah; according to all God commanded him, so did he.

Genesis 7: 1-24

1 And the Lord said unto Noah, Come thou and all thy house into the ark; for thee have I seen righteous before me in this generation.

2 Of every clean beast thou shalt take to thee by sevens, the male and his female: and of beasts that are not clean by two, the male and his female.

3 Of fowls also of the air by sevens, the male and the female; to keep seed alive upon the face of all the earth.

4 For yet seven days, and I will cause it to rain upon the earth forty days and forty nights; and every living substance that I have made will I destroy from off the face of the earth.

5 And Noah did according unto all that the Lord commanded him.

6 And Noah was six hundred years old when the flood of waters was upon the earth.

7 And Noah went in, and his sons, and his wife, and his sons' wives with him, into the ark, because of the waters of the flood.

8 Of clean beasts, and of beasts that are not clean, and of fowls, and of every thing that creepeth upon the earth,

9 There went in two and two unto Noah into the ark, the male and the female, as God had commanded Noah.

10 And it came to pass after seven days, that the waters of the flood were upon the earth.

11 In the six hundredth year of Noah's life, in the second month, the seventeenth day of the month, the same day were all the fountains of the deep broken up, and the windows of heaven were

opened.

12 And the rain was upon the earth forty days and forty nights.

13 In the selfsame day entered Noah, and Shem, and Ham, and Japheth, the sons of Noah, and Noah's wife, and the three wives of his sons with them, into the ark;

14 They, and every beast after his kind, and all the cattle after their kind, and every creeping thing that creepeth upon the earth after his kind, and every fowl after his kind, and every bird of every sort.

15 And they went in unto Noah into the ark, two and two of all flesh, wherein is the breath of life.

16 And they that went in, went in male and female of all flesh, as God had commanded him: and the Lord shut him in.

17 And the flood was forty days upon the earth; and the waters increased, and bare up the ark, and it was lifted up above the earth.

18 And the waters prevailed, and were increased greatly upon the earth; and the ark went upon the face of the waters.

19 And the waters prevailed exceedingly upon the earth; and all the high hills, that were under the whole heaven, were covered.

20 Fifteen cubits upward did the water prevail; and the mountains were covered.

21 And all flesh died that moved upon the earth, both of fowl, and of cattle, and of beast, and of every thing that creepeth upon the earth, and every man:

22 All in whose nostrils was the breath of life, of all that was in the dry land, died.

23 And every living substance was destroyed which was upon the face of the ground, both man, and cattle, and the creeping things, and the fowl of the heaven; and they were destroyed from the earth: and Noah only remained alive, and they that were with him in the ark.

24 And the waters prevailed upon the earth a hundred and fifty days.

Genesis 8: 1-19

1 And God remembered Noah, and every living thing, and all the cattle that was with him in the ark: and God made a wind pass over the earth, and the waters assuaged;

2 The fountains also of the deep and the windows of heaven were stopped, and the rain from heaven was restrained;

3 And the waters returned from off the earth continually: and after the end of the hundred and fifty days the waters were abated.

4 And the ark rested in the seventh month, on the seventeenth day of the month, upon the mountains of Ararat.

5 And the waters decreased continually until the tenth month: in the tenth month, on the first day of the month, were the tops of the mountains seen.

6 And it came to pass at the end of forty days, that Noah opened the window of the ark which he had made:

7 And he sent forth a raven, which went

forth to and fro, until the waters were dried up from off the earth.

8 Also he sent forth a dove from him, to see if the waters were abated from off the face of the ground;

9 But the dove found no rest for the sole of her foot, and she returned unto him into the ark, for the waters were on the face of the whole earth: then he put forth his hand, and took her, and pulled her in unto him into the ark.

10 And he stayed yet other seven days; and again he sent forth the dove out of the ark;

11 And the dove came in to him in the evening; and, lo, in her mouth was an olive leaf plucked off: so Noah knew that the waters were abated from off the earth.

12 And he stayed yet another seven days; and sent forth the dove; which returned not again unto him anymore.

13 And it came to pass in the six hundredth and first year, in the first month, the first day of the month, the waters were dried up from off the earth: and Noah removed the covering of the ark, and looked, and, behold, the face of the ground was dry.

14 And in the second month, on the seven and twentieth day of the month, was the earth dried.

15 And God spoke unto Noah, saying,

16 Go forth of the ark, thou, and thy wife, and thy sons, and thy sons' wives with thee.

17 Bring forth with thee every living thing that is with thee, of all flesh, both of fowl, and of cattle, and of every creeping thing that creepeth upon the earth; that they may breed abundantly in

the earth, and be fruitful, and multiply upon the earth.

18 And Noah went forth, and his sons, and his wife, and his sons' wives with him:

19 Every beast, every creeping thing, and every fowl, and whatsoever creepeth upon the earth, after their kinds, went forth out of the ark.[2]

---

[2] <u>The Holy Bible, Containing the Old and New Testaments</u>. The St. James Version, Eyre and Spottiswoode, Ltd. London.

CUT-AWAY SKETCH OF NOAH'S ARK
(Combination Exterior/Interior View)

Stern   Bow

Scale: 1/128 inch equals 1 foot.

Size: 300 cubits long, 50 cubits wide, 30 cubits high or if 24 inches = 1 cubit: 600 feet by 100 feet by 60 feet.

Dotted line at bow of ark represents the loss of space that would result if the shape of the hull was curved. It was Holly's idea to make it box-shaped.

Stern represented by "outhouse"-shaped building on the top deck: hence the name "Poop Deck" was coined by all the ark's passengers.

Bow is represented by a small "Wheel House", which is where Noah spent much of his time during the voyage. The ship's wheel did not attach to a rudder, but it still gave Noah the sense he was steering the ark anyway, until a miracle happened.

Ramp gate is seen at the stern side of the Ramp House on the top deck. The ramp itself is stored on the top deck during the voyage.

THE ARK'S HEADING TO MT. ARARAT

Mt. Ararat.

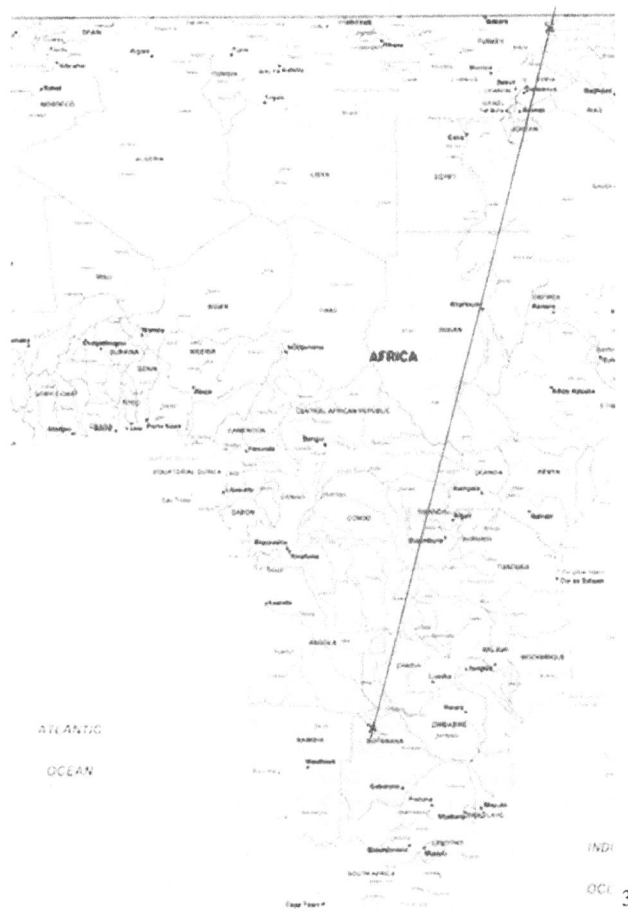

3

Nora and Noah's Farm near the Okavango Delta.
Course Heading: 12° North by Northeast.
Distance: 4,000 Nautical Miles.
Speed: 0.9 Nautical Miles/hour.
Duration Voyage: 186 days.

---

[3] Image used with permission and purchased through
http://www.dreamstime.com.

CUNIEFORM ALPHABET AND

THE EARLIEST KNOWN NUMBERS

---

[4] Used with permission from Amir Nouri:
contact@amirnouri.com

THE ARK'S "WATCH" ASSIGNMENTS

Crew Member	Voyage Day	Shift
None	1	1
Ham		2
Tam		3
Shem	2	1
Kim		2
Japheth		3
Tabeth	3	1
Nora		2
Noah		3
Merrill	4	1
Holly		2
Lance		3
Lolly	5	1
Lewis		2
Lois		3
Elliot	6	1
Elaine		2
Kelly		3
Helen	7	1
Perry		2
Terry		3
Karen	8	1
Millie		2
Todd		3
Patience	9	1
Ian		2
Fern		3
Glenda	10	1

Carl		2
Olive		3
Paula	11	1
Graham		2
Kyle		3
Bertha	12	1
Stan		2
Lily		3
Barclay	13	1
Ham		2

Etc, etc.

Merrill	190	1	Last Entry

Log Closed

"Glenda"

---

[5] Image used with permission from Anice Bommerscheim, Hoquiam, Washington.

"Graham"

"Olive"

---

[7] Ibid.

"Carl"

---

8 Ibid.

THE DELUGE.

9

INDIVIDUALS MENTIONED IN THE STORY

Name	Species	Function	Place of Origin
Noah	human	Project supervisor	Ark site
Nora	"	Supply coordinator	"
Ham	"	Noah & Nora's son	"
Tam	"	Ham's wife	"
Shem	"	Noah & Nora's son	"
Kim	"	Shem's wife	"
Japheth	"	Noah & Nora's son	"
Tabeth	"	Japheth's wife	"
Merrill	meerkat	Project shepherd	"
Holly	"	Project designer	"
Lewis	lion	Guardian/friend	Delta
Lois	"	Guardian/rescuer	"
Elliot	elephant	Guardian/rescuer	"
Elaine	"	Guardian/friend	"
Benton	buffalo	Guardian/rogue	"
Lance	loon	Messenger/friend	"
Lolly	"	Messenger/friend	"
Stan	stork	Messenger/Committee	Asia
Fran	"	Stan's partner	"
Archie	albatross	Survivor/explorer	Ocean
Alice	"	Archie's partner	"
Perry	giant panda	Committee member	"
Olive	orangutan	Committee/friend	"
Patience	peacock	Committee member	"
Karen	kudu	Committee member	Africa
Graham	gorilla	Committee/friend	"
Fern	flamingo	Committee member	"
Barclay	Barket	Committee member	"
Kelly	kangaroo	Committee member	Australia

Millie magpie   Committee/friend   "
Glenda glider   Committee/friend   "
Kyle kukuburro Committee member   "
Helen hoopoe   Committee member Europe
Todd terrier   Committee member "
Carl cuckoo   Committee/friend   "
Bertha bison   Committee member   "
Terry toucan Committee member The Americas
Ian   iguana Committee member "
Paula parrot   Committee/friend   "
Lily Llama   Committee member   "

REFERENCES

1. Celestial Navigation in a Nutshell, Hewitt Schlereth. Sheridan House, 2000.
2. The Yachtsman's Guide to Celestial Navigation, Stafford Campbell. Ziff-Davis Publishing Co., New York City, 1979.
3. Wikipedia, the free encyclopedia, "Candles", "Ruwenzori Mountain Range", "Celestial Navigation", "Magnetic Field", "Knot (speed)", "Compass", "Crux", "Jacob's Staff", "Longitude", "Sextant" and "Meerkat (Suricata)"
4. "Map of Africa"/frie_medier/dokumentasjon.htm.
5. Sun Sight Navigation, Celestial for Sailors, Arthur A. Birney. Cornell Maritime Press, Centreville, Maryland. 1984.
6. The Nature of Boats (Insight and Esoterica for the Nautically Obsessed), Dave Gerr. International Marine, Camden, Maine. 1992.
7. Deep Survival, Laurence Gonzales. W.W. Norton and Co., New York City, 2003.
8. Ceramics- A Potter's Handbook, 5th ed., Glenn C. Nelson. Harcourt Brace College Publisher, New York City, 1988.
9. The Idea of the Holy, Rudolf Otto. Translated by John W. Harvey. Oxford University Press, New York, 1958.